Daci

By

Ronna M. Bacon

2 Thessalonians 3:3. But the Lord is faithful, who will establish you and guard you from the evil one.

Psalm 91:4.   He shall cover you with His feathers, and under His wings you shall take refuge, His truth *shall be your* shield and buckler.

NJKV

Table of Contents

Chapter 1

Walking through the women's shelter, Daci Devlin smiled as she saw the debris left by the small children, just toys and books out of place. She took the time to tidy up the area and then walked towards the door. All the residents were at a picnic that had been arranged for them. The building was empty for the moment. Daci paused as she heard creaking on the stairs and frowned. There should be no one in the building.

She crept across the floors, peeking around into the hallway. There was no one there. She frowned, her deep brown eyes shadowed with worry for a moment before she shrugged and headed out of the front door, locking it behind her. Daci hesitated for a moment, not sure what had caused the noise. She shrugged before she headed for the street and her walk home.

Heading away from the shelter, Daci paused, a frown crossing her beautiful face. Her deep brown eyes searched the area before she turned back to face the shelter. She tugged at the long blond hair caught back in a braid. Something was off but she had no idea what. Daci sighed before her feet carried her back towards the house. She paused for a moment, hearing footsteps behind her. She spun to stare at the tall, good-looking man who stood there.

Dooley Cavanaugh hesitated for a moment. Someone on the streets had finally tracked him down, as late as it was in the afternoon, with the news that someone planned to bomb the shelter. He didn't believe them but knew that he had to investigate. It was what he did, investigate. Dooley worked on the drug squad for the local Oak City police department and never walked away from a tip such as this.

"Can I help you?" Daci studied the black wavy hair and deep gray eyes. She frowned. She knew this man from seeing him at church. She just didn't know his name.

"You can. You're Daci Devlin. I'm Dooley Cavanaugh." He nodded towards the shelter. "You just left there."

"I did and now I'm going back. Something is off. I thought that I heard someone inside before I left. All the residents are away at a picnic." Daci stared back at the house before she was walking rapidly back that way. She had not gone through the building and needed to before the residents returned.

Dooley stared at her in disbelief before he was running after her, a hand on her arm stopping her forward walk. She glared at him as she struggled to release her arm.

"Let me go. You have no right to stop me." Daci continued to struggle, unable to release her arm. "Let me go!"

"No! You said that you thought you heard someone in there. You are not going in there alone. Not while I'm here." Dooley just stared back at her, not really blinking. His face didn't show his emotions. He knew well enough not to show them. "I will go in with you."

"You can't. Not unless it's emergency and I really don't think that we have an emergency here." Daci was adamant about that. There was no way that she was letting him into the building. She jerked at her arm, not finding him releasing her.

"No, this is an emergency. If you heard something, then chances are someone is in there. I need to go with you. I am a police officer, Daci, even though I work on the drug squad. There is no way that I am letting you go in there on your own." Dooley stood in front of her, not moving a foot as she stared up at him.

"I can't let you." Daci's voice had dropped to a whisper. "I need to think of the ladies."

"And the ladies would accept that in this case, I do need to go with you." Dooley shot a look behind him, hearing a sound that he didn't like, a snapping sound as if something had just let go. "Daci? There is no way we're going in there. Something has happened in there." His hand on her arm turned her away from the building despite her protests.

Daci fought him, struggling to turn them back towards the building. Her face paled as she heard more snaps and then the explosion. Dooley shot a look at the building and then with an arm around Daci, he began to run from the site, Daci keeping step with him. They didn't make it very far before a large plume of smoke spiralled rapidly into the air as the house exploded. Their bodies flew through the air.

Dooley wrapped an arm around Daci and as they hit the gravel driveway, he took the brunt of the fall.

They landed in a heap, neither one moving after they landed on the ground. They didn't see the cloud grow as the house exploded. Bits of insulation, wallboard, tiles, and wood floated through the air. They didn't feel the debris as it hit their bodies, enough so that they were covered, except for one of Daci's pink running shoes that peeked out from the debris.

Sirens sounded through the air as emergency vehicles raced to the scenes. Large fire hoses were dragged across the gravel as the firefighters fought the bits of fire that were showing. Police officers draped police tape around the area.

The fire captain stood, worry on his face. He looked around as a firefighter approached him, reassuring him that everyone was out of the building as far as he knew, including Daci. He frowned. No, he decided, there was still someone here. He could feel that. He prayed for whoever it was. He had been working in the fire department for far too many years and had learned to trust those nudges that came from God.

"Search the area. There's someone here. I just pray that it's not one of the ladies."

The fire officer nodded and headed for the police officers who were watching the scene. A quick word with them had them shaking their heads before they shrugged and began to search the area. The firefighter walked towards a large pile of debris, a frown on his face. He walked around it before his steps froze. His sudden yell had heads turning his way before some of his fellow firefighters ran his way, a question called

———

through the air. He pointed to the shoe before they were working rapidly to remove the debris.

Paramedics ran that way as well, the stretcher carrying their kits bumping over the debris in their path. There just was not a clear area for them to drag it through. They waited impatiently as the painstaking removal of the debris carried on. It seemed like it was hours but was not really.

Aidan had arrived, drawing the investigation for the police department. He walked towards that activity, pausing as he saw the bodies unearthed. His hand froze as he reached to rub his face. He knew the lady. Aidan's heart dropped as he realized that it was Daci, a close friend.

"What happened?" Aidan winced as his voice sounded almost too loud in the quiet that suddenly dropped on the group.

"The house exploded. It looks as if they were running away when they were hit with debris." The paramedic looked up at Aidan before his attention was back on the couple. His head tilted for a moment. "Aidan? That's Dooley Cavanaugh. What's he doing here?"

Aidan stared at the man before he stepped to where he could assess whether it was Dooley. It was. He frowned, not sure what to think.

"They're alive?" That was his first question when he could speak.

"They are. I can't tell you how badly they are injured, but they are alive." The paramedics worked to do their assessment and then transferred the couple to backboards, neck collars in place. The officers and firefighters reached to help.

Aidan watched as the couple were rushed from the scene. He would head to the hospital shortly but for now, he was stuck at the scene. And it would take a long time to determine exactly what had happened. He reached for his phone, sending off a text message to the police chief and then asking Toryn, a close friend, to reach out to Daci's brother.

Toryn stared at his text message, his tan paling somewhat at what he was reading. On his feet, he was heading for the offices that housed the drug squad, searching for William, Dooley's supervisor. Both men stared at one another before they were out of the office and heading for the hospital, knowing that was where they were needed at the moment.

—

Chapter 2

Don Devlin ran for the emergency room, his wife, Delanie, at his side. They had been out for dinner when Toryn had reached out to him. He had been shocked to hear that the women's shelter had exploded but even more shocked and alarmed that Daci had been injured. His prayer had instantly raised for his sister. Their parents were out of town for the next two weeks, and he would be unable to reach them where they were.

Toryn turned as he heard the running footsteps, finding Don and Delanie stopping beside him. He frowned for a moment. He had been back to the examination rooms, finding the hurried activity around the couple disturbing. The physicians had not even been able to give him a preliminary report.

"Toryn? What happened? How is Daci?" Don's words tumbled over one another, not his usual calm way of talking as the head of a security team.

"The shelter building exploded." Toryn waited for their exclamations of horror to die down. "Daci's wasn't inside. It looks, from what Aidan has said, that Daci was running away. A drug officer, Dooley Cavanaugh, was with her. I'm not sure why as yet. He tried to protect her. A firefighter found them under a pile of debris. God had her one foot showing. That's the only way that they were found." Toryn watched as Don's face crumpled for a moment and then the man wrapped his wife in his arms.

"That bad? The house exploded?" Don stared past Toryn for a moment. "No one else was there?"

"No. The residents and staff were at that picnic."
Toryn's voice slowed for a moment. He had a horrible
thought that this had been a setup. "Daci? Wasn't she
there?"

"No, she had a conference call that came up
unexpectedly. She was hoping to get there once it was
over." Delanie looked up at Don. "Don? Was that a
set up? She usually doesn't have conference calls on a
Friday afternoon."

"No, she doesn't. She avoids that, just so that
she can get the paperwork done for the week." Don's
body sagged for a moment and Toryn's hand went out
to steady him. "Why this week?"

"We'll determine that." Toryn excused himself
to walk away, finding William and Aidan waiting for
him.

Don watched him walk away and then headed for
the clerk. He spoke quietly to her and then turned to
find a seat. It would be a while, he knew, his arm
wrapping around Delanie and catching her close to
him.

"We need to call the guys, Don." Delanie
reached for her phone, taking over that task.

Horror and shock greeted her as the five men
promised to be there. The five men had turned to their
wives, hugging them tightly as the ladies wept. All of
them considered Daci a sister and were terrified for
her. They just ran for their men's trucks and headed
towards where they would find Don and Delanie.

Don was on his feet an hour after he had arrived, Delanie with him, as a nurse came to find them. He drew in a deep breath even as his pleas to God raised, begging for his sister's life. He had no idea what he was facing and that terrified him. Not much did that given his line of work.

Standing beside his sister's stretcher, Don frowned as he stared down at her before his hand rested lightly on her hair. Daci was not moving and barely seemed to be breathing. Delanie's arm was around him, her soft sobs barely audible in the room with all the noise from the various equipment.

The physician hesitated for a moment, his eyes on Daci's chart, before he looked up and studied Don and then Delanie. He sighed. There was no easy way to tell them. Daci had been injured and injured badly. She would survive but she would need surgery for the punctured lung and the damage to her spleen. The physician walked towards the couple as Don turned to watch him.

"John? What can you tell us?" Don was familiar to John, having been in the emergency room too many times over the last few years.

"God had his hand on your sister, Don. She's alive and will heal. However, we do need to head into surgery with her." He detailed the injuries that needed surgery, watching Delanie as her face paled. "She's still unconscious as you can tell. I don't know when she'll rouse. For now, let's get some signatures on the consents, if you will."

—

Don nodded, reaching for the clipboard and the forms. He was Daci's power of attorney for medical reasons after his parents. He scrawled his signature and then looked back down at Daci.

"I need to find Mom and Dad." He drew in a deep breath that wavered as it happened.

"I understand. Talk to Toryn or Aidan. They can reach out to whoever it is that needs to be reached. It will go faster through official means." John walked away, heading for the nurse with the consents. He squinted at the clock. He was exhausted, having been on call for the last couple of days. God would provide the strength that he needed, that he was well aware of.

Don paced back through the waiting room, leaving Delanie sitting with the wives of his team members. He pointed to the outside and the other five men followed him. He paused, staring up at the sky. It was starting to get dark, and he felt that in his spirit. His beloved sister was seriously injured and no one could tell him why. His head dropped as he wiped at the tears that covered his face. A hand rested on his shoulder as he heard Paul praying for him. The other men picked up the prayer, bathing Daci and her family in their prayers.

"What can you tell us?" Joshua spoke up at last, sharing a look with the others.

"Daci's in surgery to repair damage to her spleen and then deal with the punctured lung. God had his hand on her." Don paused, shifting until he could look towards the hospital from where they stood under the large maple trees that lined the parking lot. "She'll be in surgery for a while. Aidan is reaching out to the police force close to where Mom and Dad are. I pray that they are reached and reached quickly."

The men with him nodded, sharing another look.

"There was someone with her?" Mark was hesitant to speak.

"There was. A Dooley Cavanaugh, Toryn said. A drug squad officer. I don't understand why, though." Don hesitated. "I'm not sure how seriously he is hurt. No one has told me." He sighed before he shifted on his feet, the cool evening breeze not all that welcome that night.

"We'll find out." Thomas walked away, heading for where he saw Aidan approaching them. His hand rose as he stopped Aidan. "Aidan? What is this about a Dooley Cavanaugh at the scene?"

"He was. We don't know why, but he was hurt as well. I can't say how bad as I don't know." Aidan looked past Thomas at Don. "How's Don?"

"Hurting. His sister is hurt and he couldn't be there to prevent it. He wants to protect her and make it better and can't." Thomas drew in a deep breath. "This Dooley? What do we know about him?"

Aidan nodded. This is what he expected from Don and his team. They would want to know what all they could find out about the man found with Daci. Aidan was well aware from how the couple was found that Dooley had done everything that he could to protect Daci. Dooley was a friend of Aidan and the

men had talked many times about how to protect the
ladies.

Chapter 3

Shifting on his hospital bed two days later, Dooley rubbed at his temple. The headache was just not stopping. He stared with frustration at the sling that encased his left arm. There had been damage done to that shoulder and arm when the debris had hit them, damage that included a fractured collarbone. He couldn't afford to be laid up at this point. Dooley had investigations that he needed to work on and that was not happening, he knew.

Looking up as he heard a tap at the door, he waved Aidan in. He was expecting Aidan to come back. He had already given what he could of a statement to him. Now, he was waiting to be discharged home.

Aidan studied his friend, a sigh rising from him. Dooley wanted to be out of there, he knew, but that would not happen for another day. Aidan had reached out to Dooley's sister, Lydia, who was also out of town and not able to return yet.

"Dooley? What else can you tell me?" Aidan waited patiently for Dooley to speak.

Dooley shrugged. He didn't know what else to say. Aidan seemed to have picked his brain clean. All he could do was thank God that Daci was alive although hurt. He looked around at the commotion that was coming from the hall. He was frowning as Aidan headed that way. Dooley slipped from the bed, finding the slippers that were waiting for him. Dooley had been able to dress and was just wanting to go home.

—

Daci stood facing Aidan, frowning at him. She didn't know him, that she was sure of. She had no idea who he was or why he was stopping her from moving forward.

"Daci? Just where are you going?" Aidan stepped back from her as she violently yanked her arm from his light grasp.

"Who are you? I'm going by you." Daci quickly slipped around him, searching for someone. Spying Dooley, she almost ran to him, finding him with his arms open to catch her. He staggered slightly, pain wafting through his body in waves as he barely kept to his feet.

"Daci? What are you doing?" Aidan approached her, reaching out to take her arm. Only he didn't manage to do that.

Daci had slipped out of Dooley's arms and hidden behind him. She peeked around Dooley, frowning at Aidan.

"I don't know who you are. Don't ever touch me again." Daci clung to Dooley's sweatshirt with a tight grasp. She raised her gaze to see another man and lady approaching her.

Aidan's hand went up to stop Don and Delanie. Don frowned at him and then at what he could see of his sister's face.

"Aidan? What's going on?" Don was puzzled and ready to reach for Daci. Only Aidan shook his head at him.

"I'm not sure, Don. She doesn't seem to know me." Aidan was perplexed by that. They were good friends, or at least he thought that they were.

"What? Of course, she does." Don moved towards Dooley, finding Dooley moving backwards as Daci pulled at him. His footsteps halted as he tilted his head to watch his sister. "Daci? What are you doing? We're here to take you home."

Daci stared at him. She had no idea whom that man was or the lady who was waiting patiently beside that other man who she didn't know. She began to shake her head.

"I don't know you. I am going nowhere with you. I'm going with this fellow." If anything, Daci's hands tightened more on the sweatshirt, almost digging into Dooley's back.

Dooley was torn. He wanted to continue to protect this lady but she had family here wanting and waiting to take her home. He didn't want her to disappear but he knew that was exactly what would happen.

"Daci? I think this is your brother. Don't you remember him?" Dooley turned as best as he could to look down at her.

Daci looked up at him, fear in her eyes as she tried to control her emotions. She had no idea whom those people were. The only one who she could remember was the man who stood in front of her.

"Dooley? Please? Don't let them take me away. I won't go with them. I need to stay with you." Daci's voice, while low, was audible to the other three. The plea for Dooley's help was clearly evident in her voice.

Don stepped backwards, finding Delanie wrapping an arm around him. He had never faced something like this. All he could do was beg God for his sister to remember who he was. And that he wasn't sure that she would do.

Aidan watched with compassion as Don struggled with his emotions and desire to protect his sister. He was well aware that Don would step back to let Daci walk away from him, no matter how much it hurt. He looked up to see Joshua, Paul, and Thomas waiting for Daci to move towards Don.

Daci continued to cling to Dooley. It seemed that he was her lifeline to what had happened to her and who she was. She didn't know the people standing in front of her and she feared them. A frown flittered across her face for a moment before she buried her face against Dooley, the fear in her just rising higher and higher.

Dooley wrapped his good arm around her despite the pain that ensued. A lady needed his help and he would not step back from her. He stared down at the head buried against him, a frown crossing his face. He prayed for this lady, who seemed to not want to leave him. Dooley could feel the chains and ice around his heart starting to free. He looked up at that point, his eyes meeting those of Don.

Don frowned at Dooley, not quite sure how to react to his sister's actions. He sighed. Even though he ran a security team, he could not force his sister to go with them. Don didn't have the heart to do that. He could hear the soft prayer that Delanie was whispering.

"She's going through one of those adventures, Don." Delanie didn't raise her voice. Only Don could hear her voice and her prayer.

"Unfortunately, I think so." Don could feel his phone vibrating in his pocket. He ignored it, his attention on his sister. "We can't stop her from leaving with him. I just don't have to like it." Don stepped backwards, taking Delanie with him. "We'll let you go, Daci. We won't stop you. This is what you need right now. Dooley, is it? Take my business card. Let me know how Daci is tonight." Don handed Aidan one of his cards who passed it on to Dooley.

Dooley took the card without looking at it, tucking it as best as he could into a pocket. He turned at that point, his arm around Daci. He walked away, his feet placed carefully on the gray tiled floor. He didn't hear any conversation behind him. His attention was on the lady who wouldn't move away from him.

Looking up, Dooley's step slowed for a moment before he nodded. His brother and sister were there, ready to take him to one of their placed. Daniel and Lydia were twins, just two years younger than himself.

"Daniel?" Dooley's voice held concern and worry.

"It's okay, Dooley. We'll head for Lydia's place. That way, your lady can get cleaned up." Daniel looked past his brother to the people standing and watching them. "What was that all about?"

Dooley stared down at Daci for a moment before he sighed and then began to pray for her.

"Daci doesn't remember her family or her friends. She only remembers me. I need to keep her near me for now." Dooley looked devastated at that. He wasn't prepared for this, he knew, but for some reason, God was deciding that he was. He could only follow the path that God had chosen for him to follow.

Chapter 4

Two hours later, Dooley walked quietly through his sister's home, his socked feet whispering against the wooden floors. He was on a search for Daci and not finding her. He paused, a hand rubbing at his shoulder to try and relieve the pain.

Daniel was watching his brother before he shook his head. He walked towards him and then touched his arm.

"In the kitchen, I think, Dooley. At least, that's where Lydia was trying to convince Daci to go there." Daniel gave a quick grin at the remembered argument between the two ladies. "I'm not sure which one would be the winner."

"I see." Dooley moved to stand just outside of the kitchen, watching the interaction between the two ladies in his life. He then walked forward, an arm out to wrap around Daci.

Daci jumped, not having heard Dooley approaching her. She stared up at him, fear on her face before it relaxed.

"You need to be lying down. You're hurt." Daci shoved at him, trying to move him from the kitchen and to somewhere he could lie down. It wasn't possible, she found. He was just not moving, Daci discovered. Her frown deepened as she continued to try and force him from the room.

"Not happening, Daci. Now, I understand that Lydia has a meal ready for us. Is that correct?" Dooley

—

turned her to the table and forced her down into a chair before he took the one beside her. He watched her, a smile lurking in his eyes.

Daci watched him, her frown still on her face. She was puzzled by the attraction that she was feeling towards him. She just didn't know if she had a boyfriend or not.

"Dooley? Should you be up?" Daci was worried about him. She had no one else to worry about or so she thought. She had set her phone on the dresser in the room that she was told to use but had not looked at it. Daci didn't want to. She was afraid of what she would discover.

"I'm okay, Daci." He reached to tuck a lock of hair behind her ear. "It's okay. We'll eat and then we can spend some time in prayer, if you would like that."

"I would. I can't remember what my life was like but I think that it included God." Daci looked sad at that.

"It is but you do have faith. I've seen you around church and have heard the testimonies from those you have helped. You are the hands and feet of God on earth." Dooley gave her a one-armed hug.

Daci leaned into Dooley, finding peace and security from his touch. That puzzled her.

Lydia curled up on the couch near Daniel. Daci and Dooley were seated on the loveseat across from them. She gave a small smirk towards her older brother before she looked at Daniel.

Daniel nodded before his head was bowed and he was praying for his brother and the lady in his life. He had no idea what had happened or why or even who. All he knew was that the brother whom he loved and looked up to had been hurt and needed healing in more ways than physical.

"Dooley?" Lydia looked back towards her brother when their time of prayer had ended. "What actually happened?"

Dooley shrugged. He wasn't sure what had actually happened. Aidan had been honest with him and told him what he knew. Aidan just didn't know what had led up to the explosion

"I don't really know, Lydia. The women's shelter just exploded. I can remember Daci talking about hearing someone inside it before she left for that day. I had to stop her from going back inside. We were arguing outside of it when it exploded. I tried to get her away but the debris and explosion hit us. I don't remember much." Dooley's eyes were on Daci, who was watching him.

"That's what happened?" Daci was shocked, to say the least. "I don't remember that."

"You're not remembering much of anything right now, Daci. Your body is reacting that way to protect you. Once healing begins, you'll remember." And Dooley was afraid that when she remembered, she would walk away from him and he would lose her forever.

"I know. And I should. You tell me that I have parents and a brother and his wife, as well as five other

---

men who treat me as their sister. I just can't remember them." Daci blinked back the tears that threatened to brim over and out of her eyes.

"And you will remember at some point. God has allowed this, Daci, for a reason." Lydia was a counsellor for youth. She knew Daci from working with her but Daci didn't seem to remember her. Lydia would not force it.

"That's what I'm afraid of. I don't know if I can handle six brothers." Daci's disgruntled words brought laughter to the room. "It's not funny. I can't imagine having six brothers."

"They look out for you, Daci." Daniel knew the men and knew their character. He knew Paul the best of them and had reached out to him just to see what he could do for Don.

"That's what I was thinking you would say. I don't want them around me. And I don't know why." Daci settled back on the couch, not realizing that Dooley had his arm around her, despite the questioning glances from his siblings.

"It is what it is." Lydia drew in a deep breath. "Your parents, Daci? They were out of town. I'm not sure if anyone has been able to reach them yet."

Daci shrugged. Not remembering them didn't mean that she didn't worry about them. She just didn't worry about them the way that she should be.

"What about your parents?" Daci looked up at Dooley, finding him watching her closely.

"Our parents? They were around when you were cleaning up. They'll be back, they promised. They had some appointments and meetings that they had to be at." Daniel was on his feet, hearing the front door. He nodded at his parents, Joseph and Leah, as they walked into the house. He kept his voice low as he spoke to them. "Dooley's in the living room. Daci's not moving from his side." He gave a quick grin at them before reaching for the bags that his father had in his hands. "I was heading to make coffee."

Joseph nodded as he headed for the kitchen. That was something that he could do and would do. Leah hugged Daniel before pausing in the living room doorway. She prayed for her oldest son and the lady seated beside him. This was far from over, she knew, and could only beg God to protect them and bring them safely through whatever this was. It had not started off all that well, she decided, before she walked into the room and hugged her son before hugging Daci, surprising that young lady.

Chapter 5

With fear on her face, Daci stared up at the lady who had just hugged her. She didn't know who she was although she seemed nice. Turning her head, she looked up at Dooley, finding his attention on the lady.

"You're here, Mom? Where's Dad?" Dooley grinned at his mother.

"In the kitchen with Daniel. You know your father. He needs his coffee." Leah found a seat beside her daughter, watching her son and the lady with him.

"I do know that." Dooley looked down at his lady. "This is my Mom, Leah. Dad's name is Joseph and he'll be in here soon." He frowned at the look on Daci's face. He was unable to read her very well.

Daci stared at the lady before she frowned. She had no idea if she had ever met her before. That frustrated her as well as frightening her deeply. Looking up at Dooley, she saw the peace and confidence on his face.

"It's okay, Daci. We'll work it through. I'll talk to the man who says you are his sister. We'll figure it out for you."

"That's what I'm afraid of. You'll figure it out, and I'll have to back my life. I'm not sure if I want to." Daci was grumbling, not sure if she meant what she had said.

There were sympathetic smiles on the faces of those around her. Joseph and Daniel had carried in

—

trays with snacks and their coffee before they found their seats. Dooley's father simply bowed his head and began to pray for his son and the lady who seemed to have become part of his life.

Delanie approached Don that afternoon, a hand resting on his shoulder. He looked up at her before an arm was out and wrapped around her, drawing her down on his knee. He was sad, he decided, and very much worried about his sister. Don had finally received confirmation that his parents had been found and that they were packing up to head home. It would take them a number of hours to reach him. They had been devastated at hearing that Daci had been hurt and had lost her memory. Don had not been able to reassure them to any extent about how she was. He couldn't as his sister was hiding from him.

"Don? What have you discovered?" Delanie's arm tightened around Don. "What can I do to help?"

"I really don't know, love, other than to pray for Daci. Aidan hasn't been able to get a lot of information yet. It's a complex investigation. Thankfully the ladies and children and the other staff were all out of the building. Barnabas Carey called and said he had a building for us to set up in again. His guys are heading this way once the scene is released in order to help with the demolition and to retrieve what we can. The ladies are as safe in the new place as they were in the old one. That's God at work."

"It is. God has provided for us in so many ways and so many times. Barnabas and his guys are certainly the hands and feet of God on earth." Delanie

———

leaned her head against him. "But what about you, Don? What can I do for you?"

Don sighed. He knew what she was asking but he had no words to say. He knew that his team and their ladies would be here shortly.

"Are we ready for the team?" Don sighed once more. He had not been sleeping, not all that well, and was exhausted.

"They're all bringing something. Toryn and Shanli are on their way. And Richard and Raleigh and their team are moving in as well." Delanie grew silent. This was not how their weekend was to have been. They had planned on leaving early on Saturday for a few days but had not even thought of that. Don had been busy with the team in for training over the day but his team had sent him home to work on Daci's troubles.

Paul turned to Don late that afternoon. He was troubled for his friend and boss. He shared a look with Mark and then approached Don.

"Don? What do you know?"

Don turned at Paul's question. He shrugged. He had found out very little about what had happened. Aidan had not had much information that he could divulge, not because he didn't want to but just because he didn't have that much information.

"Not a lot, Paul. Not a lot." Don was frustrated at that. "I've looked into Dooley but there's not a lot of information that's out there. All I know is that he is an officer but more than that I can't find anything."

"No, there wouldn't be a lot out there." Paul was frustrated as well. "What do we do? Any word from Daci?"

"Not a word. It's like she just disappeared. She's with Dooley as far as I know." Don was frustrated at that. He wanted his sister to be in his care. Only it didn't seem as if that would happen any time soon. "It's hard, guys."

"It is. I can't imagine having a family member who couldn't remember who I was." Paul rubbed at his cheek. "She's safe with him, but that doesn't make it any easier for you."

"No, it doesn't. It's hard to step back and allow her that freedom. I just wish that she could remember us. Mom and Dad were hurt at that." Don walked away at that point.

Richard appeared at Paul's shoulder, his eyes on his life-long friend. They had both faced danger with their ladies and Daci had been there helping and advising and just praying for them. He could not imagine how Don was feeling at this point.

"He's hurting, Paul. And we can't make it better. Not this time." Richard sighed. "And we want to."

"We do and we can't. Maybe one of the ladies should approach Daci. That might help."

"It might but it also might make the situation worse. Don will reach out to Dooley soon if he hasn't already done so."

"I am sure that he has already. He would not let it go so quickly or easily." Paul hesitated, opened his mouth to say something else, and then walked away, leaving Richard to stare after him before he headed to find Toryn.

Chapter 6

Four days later, Daci paced the downtown area of the town. She had had to leave the house. Dooley was hovering over her and she felt smothered. She didn't react at the smiles, waves, and questions. Daci didn't recognize the people and sighed to herself. This had not been such a good idea after all, she decided. Finding a diner, she ducked inside and just stood, not sure where to sit.

Ben watched as Daci stood just inside the door before he was beside her and with a hand on her arm, he drew her back into his office. Daci had jumped as he touched her arm and then followed him.

"Daci? I hear that you're having a bit of trouble with your memory. I'm Ben and we've been friends for years. Rachel is due in here shortly. I'll send her your way. Now, what would you like to eat?"

Daci sank into a chair. Finally, she thought, someone who wasn't demanding that she remember them or asking something from her.

"I'm not sure what to ask for. I'm sorry that I don't remember you."

"It's okay, Daci. Your memory will return. For now, let me bring you what you usually order and then if that doesn't suit you, we'll find something else." Ben walked away, troubled for his young friend. Paul had been around the night before, just to talk with him and see if he had heard anything from the street. Ben

—

had shaken his head. He had heard nothing and that troubled him.

Rachel stood for a moment before she was into the office and seated beside Daci. She watched as Daci jumped as she appeared before trying to control her emotions.

"It's okay, Daci. I'm Rachel." She grinned at her for a moment, wanting to hug the younger lady but not daring to. "What can we do for you?"

"What can you do for me? I have no idea." Daci set her plate aside, leaving part of the grilled cheese sandwich and fries on it. She wiped at the tears that overflowed and trickled down her face. "I have no idea what you can do. Do you?"

Rachel had prayed for an opportunity like that with Daci. She was prepared, she knew, to walk Daci through what she knew of her life.

"First off, finish your lunch. Then, we spend some time in prayer. And then we take a look at your life. If you're willing to do that. I won't push you." She looked around as she heard footsteps and frowned. Of course, Dooley had to show up. He would be where Daci was until Daci told him to go away. And Rachel could not see that happening.

Dooley hesitated to enter but his feelings for Daci drove him forward at last to find the chair beside her. Daci glared at him from under her eyelashes, letting him know that she was frustrated but glad that he was there. He was her lifeline right now to reality and to her faith. She was praying, begging God for relief of her lack of memory, but that wasn't just happening. Not yet at any rate.

Dooley studied his lady, seeing the emotions that she was trying hard to hide. He shared a look with Rachel, who was sitting quietly and just watching them. He hugged Daci, finding her leaning into him.

"Rachel?" Daci's voice was quiet, just underlined with fear.

"It's okay, Daci. We can still do this." Rachel was on her feet, drawing Daci to her feet as well. "Let's head for our home. We can work there. And yes, Dooley can come to." She headed for the back door, waiting for a moment before Dooley was beside her, Daci's hand tight in his.

"Let's take my truck, Rachel." Dooley pointed towards it. He waited as the ladies seated themselves before he looked around and then jumped up behind the wheel. He headed away from the diner, nodding to himself as he saw the car pulling out behind him. Dooley frowned at it before realizing that it was an unmarked patrol vehicle. His supervisor was watching out for him.

Rachel pointed towards their home office as she detoured to the kitchen and grabbed bottles of water for them all. She watched the interaction between the couple and nodded to herself. They were a couple whether or not they had accepted that already.

"Daci? What do you remember? Or can you remember anything?" Rachel sat at the desk, reaching for a pen.

Daci frowned at the questions before she shook her head.

"I'm not remembering much of anything. I don't remember the man who says he's my brother or any of the others who say they know me. I don't know if it's because I can't or because I am hiding it deep inside because of fear." She looked up at Rachel. "How do I remember?"

"Remembering is not something that you can force yourself to do. It will come with time. We can find someone for you to speak with, if that's what you want." Rachel shared a look with Dooley. "Do you have even any impressions or bits of images that you can share?"

Daci thought through that request. She had not thought about writing anything down. She reached for the pad of paper and pen that Dooley was holding out for her. Daci sighed. Dooley was doing it again, trying to take care of her. That was God's job, she decided, but she didn't know how to tell Dooley not to take care of her. She was enjoying being the centre of his attention and didn't want to be away from him. She just didn't understand why.

Her attention was on her writing, not on the quiet conversation between Dooley and Rachel. She looked up at last, before she thrust the papers at Dooley. He caught them, his eyes on her face.

"What have you remembered?" Dooley's quiet question had Daci looking at him before she looked away.

Daci shrugged, not sure that if she had really remembered anything. She had not written a lot. She wasn't even sure that what she had written would make any sense.

Dooley read through what little Daci had remembered. It wasn't a lot, he could see, and nothing that would help her recover her memory. He hugged her before he rose, drawing her up as well.

"Thanks, Rachel. Your support has helped." Dooley walked out with Daci and tucked her into his truck. He had no idea of where to head. He was due back at work the next week, on desk duty, but he didn't want to leave Daci. He watched her through the truck window, seeing how her head was moving as she searched for anyone after them.

Chapter 7

The next afternoon, Dooley walked across the parking lot at Ben's and headed into the diner. Aidan had asked to meet with him and he could not refuse, not for a fellow officer. He searched and saw Aidan in a back booth. Only he was not alone. Don was with him. Dooley sighed. He should have expected this, he thought. He remembered the lost look on Daci's face as he had walked away from her not that many minutes earlier. He could tell she felt as if he was abandoning her with his sister, and that was the farthest thing from the truth.

Sliding into the booth, Dooley sat, his eyes on Aidan. He didn't look at Don. He didn't know that man and didn't know if he ever would. For now, Dooley seemed to be the one keeping Don's sister from him.

"Dooley?" Aidan spoke at last. "How are you doing?"

Dooley shrugged, thinking through his life and emotions at that point in time.

"I don't know, Aidan. I really don't know. How am I to feel?" Dooley finally looked at Don, seeing the compassion in that man's eyes.

"About like that." Don shook his head at the question that appeared on Dooley's face. "We don't blame you, Dooley. None of us do. We blame whoever it was that caused the explosion. We blame the one behind that. You didn't do it. You tried to help from what we understand. Daci is very determined when her mind is made up and would have tried to get back into the house. You being there prevented her from dying. I don't know that we have enough information to even begin to work through this. It is going to take time." Don paused to sip at his coffee. "What can we do in the meanwhile? How is Daci?" Don was really worried about his sister. Their parents would be home that evening, and he knew full well that they would want to see Daci. Only she wasn't where she could be seen very easily.

Dooley shrugged, not sure how to answer that question.

"As well as can be expected, I think. I have tried to get her to meet with you. She's refusing but won't say why. She is terrified, I know. And she's hiding. I don't think that is who she is."

"It's not. She's an in-your-face type of personality. If a friend is hurting or needs help, she is right there. She stands up for her ladies and their children. We have taken care of them, so you can tell her that they're okay." Don stopped speaking for a moment, shock briefly on his face as he stared past Dooley.

Aidan was on his feet, heading for Daci, who stood near the counter, not sure where she should be. Daci jumped as Aidan spoke with her before she turned to where he was pointing. Seeing Dooley, Daci was across the diner and in his arms as he stood to wait for her. Don was taken aback. This was not his sister to do this but then again, the explosion and her close encounter with death had changed her. He could only

—

pray and ask God to protect his little sister when he couldn't.

Daci slid into the booth, Dooley at her side. She refused to look at the two men across from her, bringing a brief look of amusement to Aidan's face and concern and love for his sister on Don's face. Dooley watched her, sensing that she was troubled more than when he had left her just a short time ago.

"Daci? What happened?" Dooley's arm around her drew her close to him, despite the look on Don's face.

"This." Daci dug out her phone. "I got this." She swiped at her phone, unlocked it, and then handed her phone to Dooley.

Dooley didn't take his eyes from Daci as he took the phone. He couldn't. He could feel the fear in her as her body shook.

Don took the phone from Dooley's hand and read the message that was still on the screen. He grew angry at the message, his hand clenching tightly on the phone. His gaze landed on his sister and then Dooley. He was reading the man correctly. Dooley would do what he could to protect Daci. He just couldn't be with her all the time. No one could be.

Aidan reached for the phone, gently prying the phone from Don's hand. He read the text message, his face growing grim. He forwarded the message to himself and then to the lab. He knew the techs would work on it and determine what they could from it or where it had been forwarded from. At some point, Aidan would need to take Daci's phone. At this time, he could not do that to her. It was a lifeline to her remembering her past.

Dooley simply hugged Daci closer. He had glanced at the text message and he too was angry. He knew that his anger had to be given to God but for the moment, he wanted to cling to it. It gave him something to focus on.

"Daci? Have you received any other threats like this?" Aidan had gone into investigator mode.

Daci shrugged. She had no idea if she had in the past. She couldn't remember that or rather, she was choosing not to. There were images of messages floating through her mind and she just refused to think about them."

"I can't remember, Aidan. There may have been. I don't know." Her head went down on Dooley, surprise at that action on her brother's face. "When will I remember?"

"When you're ready to." Don looked out of the window, searching for the person who was watching them. He could not identify who that was. "Daci, Mom and Dad are back tonight. They want to meet with you."

Daci drew in a shuddering breath. This was what she had been expecting. She was just not ready to do that.

"Do I have to?" There was a plaintive and pleading tone to her voice.

"At some point, you will have to." Dooley shared a look with the other two men. "They need to do that, Daci, and so do you. We'll work it out. And if you will allow me to be there, I will."

"You will?" Daci raised her head to look up at him. "Yes, I need you there."

"I will be there. That I can promise you. Don will contact us and let us know when and where." Dooley could see Don nodding. "For now, let's eat as we're here and I can see Ben pulling out plates to bring this way. Just eat what you can, that's all we ask. And we are praying for you, Daci. All of your friends are and you have many." Dooley was confident on that.

Don and Aidan were nodding in agreement. They were meeting daily to do that. And they were all confident that God was in control and would protect Daci and Dooley. He had done that for each one of them.

Chapter 8

Two days later, Daci paced Lydia's home. She should be heading back to the home that they said was hers but she was reluctant to. Dooley had been staying with his sister. If she went home, then she would not have the contact with him that she had now. Daci sighed, turning to find Lydia watching her.

"Restless, Daci?" Lydia grinned at her. She had a good idea of how Daci was feeling.

"I am. I need to go home, Lydia. I'm just not ready to." Daci sighed as she flopped down into a chair. "I'm not making any sense, am I?"

"You are. You want to go home but you are afraid to. You're afraid to be on your own." Lydia bit at her lip for a moment. "And if you go home, then you don't have the contact with Dooley that you do now and what you do need. How am I doing?" Lydia grinned at Daci as she vigorously nodded.

"That's exactly how I feel. How do I do it? I know. I know. God is in control and will protect me. I just wish I could feel better about this." Daci's head went back on the chair as she stared up at the off-white ceiling.

"I have your address, Daci. I have time to take you through your house, if that's what you want and need. Dooley won't be back for a while." Lydia waited for Daci to digest her words and make a decision. It had to be Daci's decision and no one else's.

—

Daci finally raised her head, a thoughtful look on her face.

"That would work. Are we safe enough to do this?" Daci worried about Lydia's safety.

"We should be. Daniel's off this afternoon and will take us." Lydia looked around as Daniel appeared in the doorway. "You'll do that, won't you, Daniel?"

"Do what? What have you signed me up for this time, Lydia?" He grinned at his sister. This was a common question between the twins.

"To take Daci back to her home and go through it. She needs to take back that part of her life. Maybe going through it will help her remember." Lydia was on her feet, reaching for her keys and then for Daci's hand. "Come on, Daci. Let's get this over with. And if you want to continue staying with me, that's quite okay. We'll just grab some of your clothes and your Bible and whatever else you need."

Daci rose somewhat reluctantly. She wasn't sure that she was ready to do this but she could feel the nudge from God that she needed to. She walked out of Lydia's house, determined to go through her home or what everyone told her was her home and then decide what she wanted to do.

Daniel reached for the keys that Daci was holding in her shaking hand. She wasn't sure that they would even fit the lock. He smiled at her in sympathy, took the keys, and unlocked the door. He had spoken with Don and secured a password for her security system. He walked through the house, not seeing anything that seemed out of order. Daniel paused for a moment before he nodded. Her furnishings and decorations and the colour of the paint on the wall were what he had expected from what little he knew of her.

Daci stepped cautiously through the front door, standing for a moment with her eyes closed. She shook her head, not feeling that it was home. She didn't think that she would feel at home here.

Lydia waited beside her, praying for her friend. She moved to stand beside Daniel and watched Daci as she moved carefully and cautiously through the house. The twins could tell that she wasn't comfortable being there and was not recognizing anything.

Daci stood in her office, a hand on the back of the desk chair. She shook her head. She had no idea if this was her house or not. She was told that it was but she felt nothing familiar about it. She had packed a couple of duffle bags with clothes and what she needed. Daci reached for her laptop and tucked it into a bag. She had no idea why she was taking it but she needed to.

Turning back to the living room, Daci stood in front of a framed photo. It showed her, the man named Don, and an older couple. She just didn't recognize them. Daniel reached for the photo and tucked it into a bag.

"You need that, Daci. It's your family. You need to study it and come to recognize them." He was sympathetic as he spoke.

Daci nodded. That was what she had thought. She just didn't want to remember them. She only

—

wanted to be with Dooley, and she needed him right then. Except he was at work and could not be there.

Lydia hugged Daci as she locked the door behind her. She had no idea how Daci was feeling. All she could do was to pray for her friend.

"Daci? Do you need anything else?" Lydia shifted on her seat to stare into the back seat, watching Daci as she sat quietly.

Daci shrugged. She had no idea if she needed anything else. She had no inkling of what she did or didn't need.

"I don't know, Lydia. I really don't know. How do I ever remember?" Daci was almost in tears, something that she sensed was not how she usually reacted to life.

"You're hurting, Daci, in more ways than one. You're terrified. You can't remember what you need to and that worries you. You're afraid that you're hiding something that could prevent anything more from happening." Daniel gave Daci a grin in the rearview mirror. "How am I doing?"

"Spot on, I would say. I am scared and worried. I need to go through that laptop and I don't know that I have the fortitude to do so." Daci stared out of the window, not seeing the car that was following them.

"We'll work with you as we can." Lydia was determined to do that. "And you can always reach out to Don. He wants that but he understands that it has to be on your terms and in your time."

—

"I know that he wants to talk. I just don't want to." Daci grew pensive. "I somehow think that we were really close, even when he married. And the other guys? Don tells me that I look on them as other brothers. It has to hurt them that I can't remember that."

"It does but they understand. I've talked with each one of them every day as well as their wives. They are worried about you, Daci. That's a given. It's what they do. They are also trying to work through what happened but they are getting nowhere. Paul mentioned that he had reached out to a friend to help. He didn't give much more information than that."

The twins stared at Daci as she simply said the name "Emma".

"Who did you just say?" Lydia frowned at Daci. "Who's Emma?"

"Did I say that name? I don't remember her but her name brings comfort and hope. Does that make sense?" Daci didn't know if it did or not but she clung to the name that God had allowed her to remember.

Chapter 9

Don turned to face their parents, a worried look on his face. David and Deree had arrived at his place not that long ago. They were looking for Daci and shocked when he said that she wasn't with him.

"But why not, son?" David frowned at Don. "She should be. You're family."

"I know, Dad. I know. She doesn't remember us." Don had had a long conversation on the phone the night before with his parents. They didn't believe him.

"I don't know that I understand." Deree moved to hug her son before she walked away.

Don could see that his mother had pulled out her phone and sighed once more. She was trying to reach Daci, he was sure, and Daci just would not respond.

David turned to watch his wife before he turned back to Don. An arm was laid along his son's shoulders as he began to pray for both of his children. He didn't understand completely what Don was saying about Daci. He just couldn't believe that she had forgotten them.

"We need to see her, Don." David paused for a moment. "Who's running the shelter?"

"Ruth is. For now. Everyone is reaching out to help, including the ladies and children. We have them somewhere safe for now while we wait for whatever happens at the shelter address. We're not going to be able to rebuild there and keep it quiet what the building is.”

“No, we’re not.” David was on the board of the shelter and had already been reaching out to the others. “We’re working on finding somewhere to rebuild.”

“It’s not going to be easy, Dad.” Don watched his mother wipe tears from her face. “Let me call Lydia and see if we can meet with Daci. Just be warned that she won’t respond to you at all. You will need to expect her not to want to be near you. No hugs. Nothing.” Don had to prepare his parents for this. He just didn’t think that he was doing a very good job of it. All he could do was pray and ask that God lead in the encounter and heal his sister.

David was surprised at that. He had fully expected that Daci would be at home and ready to meet them.

“She’s still like that?” David wrapped an arm around Deree.

“She is, Dad. And the physician tells us that it is likely to last for a while. Daci is hiding something and this is how she is doing that.” Don walked away at that, his phone out to call Lydia. He returned as he tucked his phone back into his pocket. “Lydia says that Daci is home right now and that we’re welcome to head that way.”

Don parked his truck at Lydia’s, his eyes on the house. He was troubled by what was about to happen. He knew how Daci would react and all he could do was pray that God would lead in this situation. He knew that God was in control and allowing Daci to walk this path. He didn't understand it nor did he like it.

Lydia stepped back from the open door, watching as David, Deree, and Don approached. She met Don's glance and shook her head. Don sighed. Daci was still in that fog of forgetfulness. He didn't know what would release her but he prayed that it would be soon. This was tearing his family apart and he wanted them to heal.

Daci turned as she heard voices behind her and stared at Don. She began to frown, seeing the pleading look on his face. Her attention then went to the couple standing beside Don. Daci didn't recognize them.

"Daci?" Don approached her carefully, knowing that she would run if she had an opportunity. "These are our parents. David and Deree." He waited for her to respond.

Daci didn't recognize them or have any feelings for the couple. She made no movement towards them despite the fact that she could see how much they wanted to approach her.

"Hi." Daci's voice was low. "I'm sorry. I don't recognize you. You're my parents?"

"We are, Daci. We understand that you have a memory problem at the moment." David's voice was just as quiet and even.

Daci snorted, bringing smiles to the faces around her.

"That would be the case. I'm sorry. I really can't do this." Daci walked away, not seeing the tears on her mother's face.

"It's what she does, Dad. She walks away. We think it is more to protect herself than because she doesn't want to be hurt. I've had to step back from approaching her or being around her like I used to. She can't handle it. About the only one that she will be around is Dooley."

"Dooley?" Deree nodded. She knew the man from committees at church. "We'll take what we can. We will pray for her and for us." Deree walked away, finding Lydia waiting to give her a hug.

David reached to hug his son, feeling the emotions that Don was trying hard to combat.

"What do we know?"

"About what happened? Not a lot. There was not a lot of evidence out there. And that's frustrating everyone. I can't get a straight answer from Daci about anything. She just doesn't remember." Don was frustrated at that.

David was not aware of that and it troubled him. He walked away, heading outside, his eyes on the sky. He began to plead with God to relieve this situation and return Daci's memory. He just didn't know when that would happen. The verses that spoke of trust, peace, and protection flooded his mind, soothing his heart.

Don walked towards his father. Daci had disappeared while they had all been in the house, leaving in her car. He had no idea where she was heading but he was worried about her. Aidan had called, letting him know that a viable threat had been forwarded to the authorities, that Daci was to disappear that day and not be seen again.

"Dad? Let me take you and Mom home. Daci won't come back here if she thinks you're still here. She's not sure who to trust. The only one she trusts is Dooley. And Dooley is at work today." Don turned his father to his truck, seeing his mother waiting for them. "We'll talk, Dad. I'll talk to Daci again. Somehow, we'll get through to her."

"She's scared, son. She's hiding something and until she remembers that, we can't do a lot to help her." David helped his wife into the truck before he climbed up into it and shut the door behind him. He was more than troubled and worried about his daughter. No one could tell him why and that was what he wanted to know.

Chapter 10

Parking in her own driveway, Daci just sat and stared at her home. She knew it was hers. The address on her license told her that. She wasn't sure on that. Opening the car door, Daci hesitated for a moment. She didn't feel safe but she didn't want to be anywhere else. Aidan had sent her a text, asking where she was and was anyone with her. He passed on the news that she was expected to disappear that day. He wanted to find her and put her somewhere she could be safe. Daci ignored that text. There was no way that she was disappearing into a safe house. Don had already threatened that as well.

Standing on the front sidewalk, Daci studied the area. The lawn was cut and trimmed. Someone had done that for her. She had no idea who it had been but she was grateful. She looked around, not feeling confident that she was alone.

Hearing running footsteps behind her, Daci tried to turn but was prevented by the arms that surrounded her abdomen. Shocked, Daci didn't react for a moment. Once the shock wore off, she began to struggle, her feet kicking at the shins of the man holding her before she stomped on his feet. Her hands were flying as she fought the man. Her nails clawed at the man's face before her hands found his thumbs and pulled back on them. The man was breathing heavily from struggling with Daci. His cries of pain sounded through the air as his arms were loosened.

Daci broke from the man's grasp and ran, heading for where, she didn't know. Her feet pounded on the sidewalk as she fled. Stopping at one point, Daci turned, her hand to her throat, breathing heavily. She couldn't see the man but that didn't mean that he wasn't after her. She turned and began to run again, her head turning as she searched for a hiding place.

Ducking into a large yard on a corner lot, Daci crouched down in some bushes, her face hidden against her knees. She didn't hear anyone chasing her but she just knew that someone was. She was unable to articulate her pray but she was well aware that God heard and answered.

A hand on her arms had her screaming as she jumped. The man helped her to her feet, worry on his face.

"Daci? It's Dad. Come with me. We'll keep you safe." David had no idea why or how Daci came to be there. He was only worried about his daughter and her safety.

Daci fought him, not understanding the words spoken in fear and love that were directed at her. She broke free from David and began to run again, this time back towards her home.

Aidan paced outside Daci's home. He had headed there when she had not responded to his text messages. He was afraid for his friend. Turning as he heard a truck, he sighed. Of course, Dooley would appear.

"Aidan? Is it true?" Dooley paused his forward walk to study Aidan.

"What's true? That Daci was threatened? It is. That's why I'm here. She's not answering my text messages." Aidan was frustrated and worried by that.

"She won't. She doesn't remember you and doesn't know if she can really trust you. It's how it works." Dooley looked around. "Her car's here."

"It is and so was a man who I suspect was trying to abduct her. He's in custody and will be interviewed by another detective." Aidan pointed towards her home. "I don't think that she made it inside at all."

"No, I doubt that she did." Dooley looked around as he heard running footsteps and then felt a body hit him. His arms closed around Daci as she buried herself against him as hard as she could.

Daci couldn't or wouldn't speak or move away from Dooley. He was her safety line and she needed that right now. She was terrified and didn't know where to go or who to turn to.

"Daci? What happened?" Dooley's voice was quiet and even. "Talk to me, love. Tell me what happened."

Daci was shaking her head. She didn't know if she had the words to do that.

"Someone tried to take you from here?" Dooley waited patiently until he felt her nod. "You ran?" Again, Daci nodded. "Did you find somewhere to hide?"

"I did. The man who found me there seemed to know me. I didn't know him." Daci refused to look up, not seeing David standing nearby.

Dooley studied David, seeing the raw emotions on the older man's face. His eyes slid closed even as he heard Aidan asking David questions. He didn't focus on them. He focused on Daci.

"Daci? Come on." Dooley nudged her towards his truck and then lifted her up onto the seat. He stood where he could watch her, his back to the open truck door. "Do you want to speak with your father?"

Daci's eyes slid closed and tears tracked down her face. She felt Dooley's hand on her face wiping them away.

"No, I don't. I want to run away, Dooley. I want to leave this town and never come back. Only I can't do that."

"No, you can't, Daci, but you can run towards me." Dooley waited patiently for Daci to digest what he said. Her eyes popped open as she stared at him. "I mean that, Daci. Run to me. I'll do what I can to protect you. I would marry you today to do that."

Daci's mouth opened and closed a few times. She swallowed hard, not sure that she had heard him correctly.

"You would marry me? I can't remember anything. That wouldn't work." Daci felt a ray of hope in Dooley's words.

"I do mean it. And we'll make it work. I have been praying for a way to protect you, and God laid this on my heart. Only if you want." His finger rested on her mouth. "Pray about it, Daci. For now, Aidan does need to speak with you."

———

58

"But do I want to speak with him?" Daci studied Aidan before she sighed. "What do you want, Aidan?"

Aidan grinned at her for a moment before he sobered. He did need to speak with her, to find out what had happened.

"What happened today, Daci? What can you tell me?"

"What happened? I was just standing in my own yard when someone grabbed me from behind. I fought him and when I could, I ran. I have no idea where I ended up but the man who tried to help, I guess it was, but that scared me. I ran back here. Who was that who was here?"

"That man is under arrest. I was here, I guess, just after you escaped. You beat him up pretty good." Aidan grinned at the look on her face. "You put your training to use, Daci. It's exactly how you should have reacted. Where you ended up? That was at your parents' home. You ran there on instinct, knowing that they would protect you."

"I ran that way? I really don't remember. I was just in a fog at that point. I don't remember anything until I found Dooley." Daci looked up at Dooley. "I really don't know who it was or why."

"It's okay, Daci. We have the man in custody. We pray that he'll talk but we don't know if he will. For now, go with Dooley. He's heading back to the detachment. You'll be safe there." Aidan nodded at Dooley before he walked away, a hand out to draw David away.

Dooley shut the truck door and then walked slowly around the truck to climb in. He hesitated to drive away, his eyes on Daci's home. Would she ever remember? He begged God for that and for God to protect her.

"Where do you really want to go, Daci? I do have to go back to work." Dooley rubbed at his shoulder, finding the pain almost too much at that point.

Daci shrugged. She had no idea where she wanted to go or where she should be. God alone knew that and He was not telling her.

Chapter 11

Dooley studied the paperwork in front of him without really taking in what it said. He was frustrated. He could not be out on the streets as he should be. The paperwork that he was doing didn't make a lot of sense without that. He sighed as he sat back in his chair. Dooley's eyes found Daci as she slept. She had stretched out on the couch in his office. He had awkwardly covered her with a blanket using only his good hand. That hand had rested on Daci's hair for a moment as he prayed for her. That faith was what he knew would get them through.

Walking away from his office, Dooley hesitated for a moment. He needed to go somewhere but he had no idea where that was. He looked up as he heard William's voice.

"Dooley? Do you have a moment?" William pointed to an empty conference room. "I need to talk with you about something."

"Sure. I needed a break anyway." Dooley perched on the edge of a table. "What's up?"

William rubbed at his neck. He wasn't sure how to broach the subject with Dooley that he needed to.

"Dooley? How long will you be laid up?"

Dooley shrugged. He really didn't know.

"Another four or five weeks in the sling. Then a number of months in physiotherapy. There is no guarantee that the arm will ever be the same. And that impacts my work."

"It does. You are a valued member of our drug squad, but you're not able to do your work at the present time. John has asked if you would transfer on a temporary basis to the cold case squad. That would keep you busy but also help them out as well." William waited for Dooley to respond.

"The cold case squad?" Dooley shrugged. "It would work. I need to pray over it, though."

"Do that. Come and see me when you've prayed it through." William walked away, hesitating outside of the room to pray for his officer.

Dooley sat for a while, lost in thought, before he was on his feet and headed back to his office. He watched as Daci continued to sleep. John's request had come out of the blue but it really was in line with his interests. He looked up, thanking God for the proposed opportunity. He certainly felt that he would take the transfer. The drug squad was wearing him down and burning him out.

Daci roused thirty minutes later. She frowned as she stared at the desk and the pair of feet that she could see under it. She had no idea for the moment where she was. Sitting up, Daci looked around, confused as to where she was. She jumped as she heard footsteps and then someone sitting beside her.

She looked up, frowning at Dooley before her face cleared. She leaned into his hug, feeling safe and cherished even though her mind was telling her that was far from the truth.

—

"Daci?   Have a nice sleep?"   Dooley smiled down at her, a smile just for her.

"I guess that I did.   Thank you."   Daci looked around once more, taking the bottle of water that he handed her.   "What have you been up to?"

"Just working."   He glanced at his watch.   "I can pack up and leave, Daci.   How be we head to Ben's for a meal?"

"That sounds good.   I just need to freshen up a bit."   She was on her feet and heading for the ladies' washroom.

Dooley reached for Daci's hand as he helped her from his truck and didn't release it.   He could feel the tingling on the back of his neck and knew that someone or more than one person was watching them.   He refused to lend credence to their observation by looking around.

Daci leaned back in the booth as they finished their meal, her eyes on the outside.   She could see the pedestrians walking by but one man seemed to be lingering as if waiting for someone.

"Dooley, there's someone out there.   The man in the blue hoodie.   He's not leaving but seems to be too interested in the building."   Daci nodded towards him, feeling more confident in her observations and in expressing them.

Dooley shot the man a look and nodded. He was a known drug dealer and that worried Dooley.   His phone was out as he called for assistance, describing and also naming the man.   Daci and he waited for the apprehension of the man. That happened quickly, even though the man put up a fight.

Daci watched with interest as the man was arrested before she frowned at Dooley. She had recognized the name that he gave. She knew that name and who was behind him. Not much like that passed by her.

"Dooley? He's behind this?" Daci's face was white with fear.

Dooley shrugged. He didn't know for sure but with that man showing up as he did? It was highly likely that he was or someone he knew was.

"I don't know, Daci." He was on his feet, pulling her to hers before he walked them out of the diner. Ben waved as he did so, knowing that Dooley had not paid but that it was just okay. The most important thing was to get Daci to safety. Only Dooley was in danger too. No one could figure out why. As Aidan had said, there was just not enough information to determine the who or why.

Lydia watched late that evening as Daci paced her home. She sighed. Something had happened and that something was going to cause Daci to run. And run she couldn't do. Dooley would go after her, Lydia was certain of that.

"Daci?" Lydia patted the couch seat beside her. "Come and sit. Talk to me. Tell me what's wrong."

Daci dropped in a chair opposite her friend. She had no idea what was wrong other than her memory was not returning and that Dooley had proposed to her.

"I don't know. I can't remember those people who I should. Someone tried to kidnap me today from outside of my home. I'm being followed." She blinked back the tears. "And Dooley proposed to me."

Lydia stared at her, listening to her words, and then blinking at Daci's last statement. Dooley had proposed? Lydia was shocked at that but then as she thought through it, it didn't surprise her.

"Daci? Dooley proposed?"

"He did." Daci was troubled by that. She didn't want him to be harmed but at the moment, it seemed the only route that she could take. She was troubled by that and could only trust God to deliver her from her troubles. God knew that path that she was walked, had known since time began what she would face.

—

Chapter 12

Dooley rammed his front door closed as hard as he could, leaning on it with his back, trying to reach for the lock with his good hand. He felt the door slamming into his back as the men banged viciously at it. The door flew open at last, sending Dooley flying towards the floor. He landed awkwardly on his good side, a hand grabbing at the other arm, trying to protect his injured shoulder as best as he could.

Unable to prevent the blows delivered on his body, Dooley lay quiet at last. He didn't hear the men leaving or feel the paper that floated down to land on his body. He didn't hear or feel anything, the blows taking away his consciousness. He didn't move for a number of hours, not until Daniel tapped at his door, Caleb at his side and then entered, surprised that the door was open.

Daniel reached for the light switch, flipping on the lights both outside and in the hallway. He looked around, hearing Caleb's shout and saw the man leaping forward. His eyes dropped to find his brother lying motionless on the floor. He was on his knees beside Dooley, reaching for his wrist and then for the letter. He set the letter to one side as he worked on his brother.

Caleb was on his feet, calling for assistance, and then heading through the house and then outside. He didn't see anything but then it was dark and he did not have a powerful enough light to see much.

Aidan stood and watched as the paramedics worked on Dooley. He had not expected to be called to Dooley's house for such an event. He reached out to Lydia, letting her know that Don would be there to pick up both Daci and herself. Dooley had been injured and he would need Daci with him.

Daniel had called their parents, just asking that they meet him at the hospital, that Dooley had been injured once more. He heard the suppressed sob in his mother's voice before he clicked off the phone. He watched as his brother was transferred to a stretcher and the stretcher to a paramedic rig. He walked after it, his hand on his face as he prayed for Dooley. He had no transportation to the hospital, climbing up into the back of the rig as he was pointed to and then motioned to do that.

Aidan was frustrated. There was just no evidence as to why Dooley was attacked. He had no idea why it had happened or who had done it. The security system would be looked at but he was not hopeful that it would help.

Daci stared at Lydia in horror as she told her what had happened to Dooley. Daci reached for her phone and tucked it into a pocket as she ran for her car, Lydia calling out for her to wait, that someone was on their way to take them to the hospital. Lydia ran after her, the front door locked behind her, and slid into Daci's car just in time. Daci drove off as rapidly as she could, fearing that she would be too late to find Dooley, that he would be dead and it would be her fault.

David reached for his daughter, stopping her forward run. She struggled to escape him, her hand hitting him in the face. The unexpected blow loosened his grip and Daci ran from him, heading for the clerk. She turned away to find Lydia and Daniel standing with her. Daniel reached to hug her before he directed them to a chair. David and Deree sat nearby, shocked at the violent way that their daughter had reacted.

Daci sighed. She didn't want to be there. She wanted to run, and she was well aware that was not her, that she would stand and face whoever or whatever it was that threatened her.

Joseph and Leah found their son in the emergency department, not aware that Daci was there with their other children. They had been taken back, distraught at how they found Dooley. He didn't respond to their touch. Turning away, they were sent to the waiting room as Dooley was being assessed. Neither one saw the number of officers who wandered around the area and inside and back outside. They found their children, not surprised that Daci was there.

Hours seemed to pass although it really hadn't been that long. The nurse nodded as Aidan approached the room, pointing into it. He found the physician there, just finishing his assessment.

"Doc? What can you tell me?"

The physician turned to him, shaking his head.

"What happened, Aidan? He's been beaten again. We're working him up, imaging, blood work, etc. But he's not rousing." The physician was somewhat concerned about that.

"No, I wasn't expecting him to. Has his family been back?"

"His parents have been. Who else is out there?" The physician looked over his reading glasses as Aidan hesitated to speak.

"His brother and sister. And the lady that he's interested in."

"A lady? Do I know her?"

"Daci Devlin."

The physician paused. He nodded after thinking that through.

"Daci? She was injured a while ago. The same time as Dooley, if I remember correctly."

"That's correct. Dooley is Daci's lifeline right now. She can't remember anyone or anything but him. I think she's burying everything to protect herself. And that's not her."

"No, it's not. I've worked with her many times with her ladies and their children. She's fierce with protecting them. But it's difficult when she's on the other side of the coin and a victim."

"More than likely." Aidan stood and watched Dooley. His friend and fellow officer was not responding.

Dooley's parents and his siblings stood around his bed thirty minutes later. Lydia had kept a hand on Daci and pulled her with them. They were not surprised that he didn't respond to any of his family, having been warned that he was not responsive. Daci had hesitated to come with them. The family left at last, leaving Daci with Dooley.

Daci reached for his hand, not expecting him to respond. She jumped as his hand moved and then covered hers, the grip strong. She watched as his eyes flickered and then opened. She barely breathed as she could see him searching the room and knew the moment that he found her.

"Daci? You're okay?" Dooley moved restlessly on the bed. "I was afraid for you."

"I'm fine but you're not." Daci's free hand landed on his chest. "You need to stay still, Dooley."

Dooley was shaking his head. He sat up despite her protests. He reached to wrap her into his arm. His head rested on the top of her head. Dooley wanted to protect her. Only it didn't seem as if that was going to be possible at all.

Daci stood for a moment before she looked up at him.

"Dooley? Were you serious when you asked me to marry you?"

Dooley nodded but knew that this was not the time for that. Daci was just not ready for that.

"I did, but you're not ready for that. Not yet." Dooley kissed her forehead. "I'm ready to leave, sweetheart. Daniel would want me to go with him."

"I know that he does and so do your parents." Daci sighed. "And the people who say that they are my parents are out there. I just don't remember them. When will I?"

Chapter 13

Daci's parents watched as she walked away with Dooley, her hand in his. Daci had spoken briefly with them before she had turned to him. They were at a loss as to what to do. Joseph had stopped beside them.

"Dooley's at Daniel. Daci and Lydia will likely head that way. We'll get you all together tomorrow. I know that is hard."

"That would be nice. Thank you, Joseph. We'll head there." David paused, a thought crossing his mind. "What are your thoughts on all this?"

"My thoughts?" David shared a look with Deree. "Listen, why don't we find some place to get a coffee and discuss this?"

"That sounds good. How about Ben's?" Deree walked away with David, leaving Joseph and Leah following them.

The two sets of parents spent an hour together, just discussing what they knew or didn't know and what they could do. They came to the conclusion that they really didn't know much or had any suspects.

Dooley sank into a chair, his head buried into his hands. He ached all over and didn't want to move at all. His shoulder was paining him more than it had been. Dooley felt a hand on his shoulder and then Daniel's voice praying for him. He could hear the conversation in another part of the house and then more footsteps. He sighed. He wanted to be on his own or with Daci and that was not happening.

—

Daci watched Dooley, a frown on her face. She had no idea what had happened and she needed to know that. She turned to find Aidan standing near her.

"Aidan? What happened?" Daci moved away from the kitchen as Aidan pointed towards the front door. Once outside, she stood, watching him.

"This was deliberate, Daci. I don't know if you're remembering anything at all but you need to. We can't go forward much without your input." Aidan was stern. "There was a letter. Daci, it threatened Dooley with death unless you cooperate. How do we do this?"

"I don't know. I really don't know." Daci found Don standing near her, a worried look on his face. "Don? I don't remember you." She ran from them, heading for her car and home. She locked the door behind her. She sank down with her back to the door, her head buried against her knees. She sobbed, everything just too much for her at the moment. Daci ignored the chiming of her phone. On her feet, she ran for her bedroom and just threw herself across her bed, sobs continuing to shake her body. Her emotional storm finally eased as she slept, the occasional sob still shaking her body.

Don watched as Daci ran from him, sorrow on his face. He wanted to help his sister but he didn't know how to. They were close and always had been. Don turned as he heard a voice beside him.

Dooley stood there, rocky on his feet, watching Daci leave. He didn't want her to, but he understood why she did.

"She's hiding, Don. And I can understand why she wants to." Dooley's words didn't bring any comfort to Don.

"I know. I wish that she wouldn't."

"With her lack of memory about you all, she's not sure who she can trust. In her heart, she knows that she can trust you. Her mind is what is causing her to hesitate and run." Dooley waited patiently for Don to speak. He shared a look with Daniel.

"That's about it, isn't it? All we can do is pray that God restores her memories. I just wish it was now. It hurts, you know?" Don was having trouble controlling his emotions. And not one person blamed him. "I know that God is in control and that He has laid out the path that she's walking. Doesn't mean that I have to like it." Don walked away, leaving the brothers to stare after him.

"No, it doesn't mean that you have to like it but you do have to live it." Daniel hesitated before he walked away as well.

The next morning, John headed through the police department, looking for Dooley. Dooley had been transferred to the cold case squad and was settling in somewhere. John paused at a small conference room and watched Dooley working away. He approached him, pulling out a chair to sit beside him.

"Dooley? What file are you working on?" John studied Dooley carefully, seeing the pain that the younger man was trying hard to hide.

"The Evans one. It has bothered me for a while that we could never solve it." Dooley sat back in his chair, his eyes on the file in front of him. "What do you know about that?"

"Not a lot. It was on the books before I joined the squad. At least fifteen years. You would have heard about it."

"I did. I was a teen when the murders happened. I didn't realize that it had been so long." Dooley tapped at the folder. "I need to read through this a few times and then look at the evidence. I'll be speaking with whoever is still around."

"Do that. And if there are retired officers, speak with them as well." John hesitated. "Are you okay with this, Dooley?"

Dooley studied his folded hands before he nodded.

"I am, John. I truly am. I was getting restless with the drug squad. It really didn't fit me all that well."

"No, it didn't. You worked well there, Dooley, but your heart was not totally in it. This suits you better." John was on his feet and moving on, having a meeting to get to.

Dooley studied the folders in front of him before he too rose as well, locking the door behind him. He walked from the building and through the downtown. He didn't know exactly where he was heading until he found himself standing and staring through the temporary fence that surrounded the old shelter. Was there a connection between the cold case and the explosion?

Dooley looked up, praying for a resolution. God was in control, that he had to acknowledge. He was their shield and protector. He hid them in the hollow of the rock and covered them with His wings. Dooley felt peace at last, no matter that the adventure was not over.

Chapter 14

Walking towards the shelter, Daci's feet slowed. She was not sure that she wanted to be there but she felt that she had to be. She studied the area before she noticed that Dooley was standing there, his hands clenching at the wire fence.

Daci stopped beside him, an arm around him. She felt his arm around her as he swept her close to him. She had no idea why he was there or even why she had appeared.

"Dooley? What are you doing here?" Daci finally broke the silence around them, the silence except for the sounds of nature and of the nearby traffic.

"I don't know, Daci. I really don't know. I am working on a cold case and it led me to here." He laid a cheek against the top of her head. "What are you doing here?"

Daci shrugged. She really wasn't sure why she was there other than that God had directed her steps that way.

"He did, did He? And we do obey Him when He directs us like that. Has any of your memory come back?" Dooley waited patiently for her to speak.

Daci shrugged. The images were coming faster and were clearer. She just didn't know if they were the truth or just her imagination.

"I think that it is, but I can't say for sure. It's frustrating, Dooley, just so frustrating." She hugged him tighter, feeling safe and cherished standing with him. "This building? I wish that this had not happened. It has disturbed so many lives. I wish that I could remember the ladies. Lydia took be my the new shelter yesterday. I didn't remember the staff or the residents. That hurts." Daci wiped at a tear that had escaped.

"I know that it does love. I really do." Dooley moved away from the fence, turning them to walk away. His movement stopped as he saw the five people standing in front of them.

Daci stared at the five, a frown on her face. She thought that she should recognize them. The tall man in the centre had a smile on his face. He was flanked by two ladies and they were flanked by two men.

"Daci? I know that your memory isn't what it should be. I'm Richard. On my right are Silver and Joseph and on my left Naomi and Stephen. We are friends. In fact, you, Don, and I grew up together as neighbours. Don asked if we could stop by and just talk with you, see if maybe our faces would trigger your memories." He continued to grin at her, the ease of old friends in his demeanour.

"I'm sorry. I am sure that we are friends, but I don't remember you. And I should." Daci was sober as she spoke. "What else are you here for?"

Richard laughed. This was just so Daci, he decided, not letting him away with anything.

"Just to make sure that you two stay safe. Don asked that. He has also called in Abe to help. Abe has a security team as well, Daci, as you won't remember that."

Dooley had been listening quietly as Richard spoke before his attention was caught by men walking towards them. He frowned. They were in law enforcement, he decided, not sure what to make of them.

"Richard? This Abe? Was he heading here today?" Dooley nodded behind Richard.

Richard turned and began to laugh harder.

"He wasn't but he is here. Daci, this is Abe and his team. Now, what do we do with you two?"

Dooley shrugged. He needed to be back working on that cold case, but he didn't want to leave Daci. He simply reached for her hand and pulled her with him, walking past Richard and his team and then Abe and his team.

The two teams stared after them before they turned to look at one another. Abe shrugged, a grin on his face before he walked closer to Richard.

"She still can't remember?" Abe's voice was kept low. He could feel the watchers out there and turned to search for them. He didn't see them and suspected that they had followed the couple.

"No, she can't. At least, that's what she's saying." Richard was very worried about his friend. It was so dangerous for anyone who could remember. He

---

just didn't know how it would work for someone who couldn't.

Daci walked through her home that night, pacing, restless, and uncertain as to what she faced. The images of what she suspected was her life were beginning to come fast and furious and that scared her. She was in constant prayer for peace and safety. Daci knew in her heart that God was protecting her. She was also enough of a realist to know that He allowed danger and harm sometimes in His children's lives.

Staring at the envelope that had been taped to her door, Daci paused, her arms wrapping around herself. She didn't want to open it but she knew that she had to. A finger traced the scrawled letters that spelt out her name, the red ink garish on the white envelope.

Daci opened the envelope carefully, not sure what she would find inside. A single note card fell out. She stared down at the blank side of it before her finger flipped it over. She frowned at the red ink that once more covered a white paper, this time a blank note card.

"It is better if you never remember."

Daci shuddered with fear. Someone knew that she couldn't remember and that had to be someone close to her. She had no idea who it would be. Her phone was out to take a photo of the card and then to send it on to Aidan. Her actions were automatic as she did so, not realizing that she was reacting as she normally would.

Hearing the doorbell, Daci jerked back to the present, her eyes huge with fear. She crept to the door, staring through it. She frowned as she opened the door, facing Aidan. Aidan was angry, she could see.

"Daci? Where is it?" Aidan stalked into the house, searching for the letter.

"It's on the kitchen table." Daci followed him, watching as Aidan read the note and then turned back to her. "Daci?"

Daci shrugged. She had no idea who had sent it or even when it had hit her mailbox. She had not checked for mail the day before.

"I have no idea, Aidan. Can you explain it?" Daci was not backing down from him. She was beginning to remember him and knew just how stubborn he could be. She just didn't tell him that.

"No, Daci, I can't. And I know that you can't either. You're not the one sending this to yourself. It's not you or your character." Aidan turned to watch her. "Have you remembered anything at all?"

"Bits and pieces. Not enough to know what is truth and what is a dream." Daci was saddened at that. "I really do want to remember, Aidan, but I think that I'm not remembering because I'm afraid to."

"That is highly likely, Daci. Have you found somewhere to talk with?" Aidan was concerned for her.

"I have." Daci pointed to the note. "What do we do with that?" She pointed once more at the note.

Chapter 15

Dooley walked towards Daci that evening, finding her sitting on her front porch. She just looked up at him as he sat beside her, their shoulders touching. She was frustrated and angry and knew that if she spoke, Dooley would bear the brunt of that. Instead, Daci just sat, content to be outdoors and with Dooley. She couldn't understand that, not realizing that she had fallen in love with the tall man who shared her space that night.

Watching her closely, Dooley was well aware that something had happened that day. He didn't pry. He was also content just to sit beside Daci, knowing full well that he was in love with her and wanted just to be with her.

"What happened, Daci?" Dooley finally had to ask.

"What happened? Dooley, how can you ask that?" Daci stared at him before she thrust her phone at him. "This happened. Who did this?"

Taking the phone, Dooley was troubled by how much it was shaking. He looked down at the photo of the note. Frowning, he kept reading it before he looked up at Daci. He could see the fear that she was trying had to tamp down but was not very successful at that.

"Daci? When did you get this?"

"This morning. Aidan took it. We have no answers as to who or why." Daci leaned against him, seeking comfort and protection from him.

—

"I don't understand. Not yet." Dooley was puzzled at the note. Who didn't want Daci to remember? "Have you any idea who it was?"

Daci shook her head at him. She had no idea who it might be.

Rising at last, Dooley tugged Daci to her feet and then up on the porch. He wrapped her in a hug and prayed for her before waiting until she had entered the house and closed and locked the door. His hand rested against the door for a moment before he walked away. Dooley was highly troubled about the note. Checking his watch, he sighed. He couldn't talk with Aidan but he would find him tomorrow.

The next day, Aidan stared up at Dooley as he stood in front of his desk. He dropped the pen that he was holding onto his desk.

"You've talked with Daci." His words were a statement and not a question.

"I did, Aidan. She is terrified. And so am I. Who is doing this to her? And who tells a victim not to remember?" Dooley's hands waved. "I know. I know. We see it all the time." Dooley was frustrated, however. He wanted to protect his lady and didn't know how to, even though he was a police officer.

"We do, Dooley. That we do." Aidan studied his friend. "What are your thoughts?"

"My thoughts? About all this?" At Aidan's nod, Dooley shrugged. "I have no idea what to think. If it was a case that I was investigating, I know what I would do. But I'm not the investigator."

"No, you're not. You have thoughts though."

"I do." Dooley reached into his shirt pocket and pulled out a folded sheet of paper. "These are my thoughts, Aidan. I'm not sure if any of them are valid. But work with them. Talk to me as you need to."

Dooley was on his feet and headed for the conference room. He unlocked the door and then stood, staring at the file boxes on the table and then at his notes on the white boards. He didn't feel like working on this case but he would. There was something about this case that read wrong to him and he wanted to find out what was wrong. It was in his nature to continue to push.

Sitting at the table, Dooley's head dropped. He began to pray and then sat silent before his God, waiting for peace and comfort to fill his heart. When he did, he looked up and mouthed a thank-you to his God. Turning his attention to the work in front of him, Dooley was soon immersed in his work. He didn't hear anyone moving around him and looked up in surprise to see Toryn watching him.

"Toryn? How long have you been here?" Dooley sat back, his pen still in his hand.

"Not long. You were deep in your study of that case. What are you finding?" Toryn pushed somewhat for Dooley to react.

"What am I finding? I am finding information that was never followed up with. There is evidence here that was never looked at. How did that happen and get past everyone who has looked at this case?"

—

"For starters, this case has never been looked at since the initial investigation. We have confirmed that. That should not have happened."

"No, it shouldn't have. I looked up the officer who did the investigation." Dooley hesitated to say anything. "He's not around any more but from what I understand, he didn't have a good reputation in the city."

"No, unfortunately, he didn't. We need to rectify the fact that this murder was never solved and bring closure to the family." Toryn hesitated to continue. "Work on it as you can. Reach out to who you need to. And bring in the techs as you work through this." Toryn was on his feet, walking away, confident that the murder would be solved and Dooley would be the one to do that.

Dooley looked after Toryn before he turned his attention back to the report that he had been engrossed in when the chief had appeared. He frowned at one sentence before he was on his feet to copy that page. Back in his chair, he studied that page. A thought of what he had seen in the boxes sent him searching for another folder. Opening it, his finger traced the information before he was looking back at the photocopier. He sat back, lost in thought for a moment before he was on his feet and locking the door after him. Dooley needed to talk to someone and that someone was Ben.

Ben looked around as he heard Dooley speaking with him and then just pointed towards his office. Ben had been worried about Dooley and Daci. This would

—

give him an opportunity to assess for himself how Dooley was.

"Dooley? You're troubled, son. What is it?" Ben sat in a chair beside Dooley. "Let me pray with you first."

Dooley nodded, needing those prayers. His thoughts shifted to Daci for a moment and prayed for his lady. Things were changing and he didn't know if they would stay a couple, if that's what they already were.

"I am, Ben. In more ways than one." Dooley bit at his lip, not sure how to proceed. "Ben, this is your town. You hear so much from the street. What can you tell me about the Evans' murder?"

Ben nodded. Finally, he thought, someone is looking into it.

"The Evans' murder? That goes back a lot of years. It was never really investigated, not that I recall." Ben rubbed a finger on his cheek. "Mrs. Evans has passed away but we did talk a lot. She always suspected that her son or his friends had something to do with that but she had no real evidence. The son, Joe, is still in town but he is not very well liked at all. The rumours have always been there that he was behind the murder. No one could ever prove it, though."

Dooley was taking notes, asking the questions that should have been asked all those years ago.

"So, you think it was the son?" Dooley was careful how he worded his question.

"That's what we have all thought, Dooley. Now, it's up to you to prove it." Ben reached for a piece of paper and scrawled some names down on it. "Talk to these people. They may not want to talk, depending on how scared they are of Joe Evans." Ben studied Dooley for a moment. "The women's shelter? That was a home that the Evans owned before Mrs. Evans donated it. There may be a connection there. If I remember correctly, that's where the older Evans were living when he was killed." Ben watched with sympathy as a shocked look crossed Dooley's face.

Walking back towards his office, Dooley was lost in thought. Ben had been a source of information, just as he knew that he was. He needed to speak with someone who had been on the force at that time and could provide any information that they would. He just didn't know who to go to.

Aidan was waiting for Dooley as he approached the steps to the building. His hand stopped Dooley before he had climbed any of said steps.

"Dooley? I need to talk with you and I want to do that away from here." Aidan pointed towards his car. "In."

Dooley shot him a startled look before he did just what Aidan had ordered. And it was an order and not a request. Dooley watched carefully as Aidan drove away, knowing that his friend and fellow officer would not have taken this step if he had not felt it necessary.

"Aidan? What's going on?"

"Dooley? Where were you just now?"

"At Ben's. I had some questions about that cold case. The Evans' murder." Dooley didn't look at Aidan. Instead he stared out of the window, not sure what to think or believe any more.

Aidan nodded. He had been told that Dooley was working that case.

"And what did you find out?"

"That the shelter was where the Evans lived when he was killed." Dooley heard the exclamation from Aidan. "Aidan?"

"I don't know if we had that information, Dooley. I didn't know that. That changes things, you know?"

"I know. I wasn't working on that case at the time. So how does this all fit together?" Dooley was at a loss. "I need to speak with Daci about this, but I'm not sure how much she will remember."

"There's that. Something at some point will trigger her memory." Aidan was afraid for his friend, knowing that she needed to but she just wasn't remembering, or if she was, she was not telling him.

"That's what I'm afraid of. That she will find herself in danger and that will trigger her memory. I worry around her almost too much." Dooley stood and walked away, leaving Aidan staring after him, a concerned and sympathetic look on his face.

Dooley turned as he heard his name. Don and Joshua were walking towards him. He sighed. He needed to be back in the office but that didn't seem to be happening right at the moment.

"Dooley? How are you?" Don was concerned about the man who was closer to his sister than he was at the present time.

Dooley shrugged. He had no idea how he was to feel.

"I have no idea. Don? Joshua? I don't think that you're here just to shoot the breeze."

—

"We're not here just for that. We do need to speak with you. Do you have time right now?" Don waited for Dooley to respond.

Dooley shook his head.

"Not at present. I'm deep into an investigation that I need to continue. How about tonight?"

Don nodded. He had expected Dooley to respond that way. He shared a look with Joshua.

"We can do that, Dooley. We'll be at your house tonight. We're not letting you get away without talking to us." Don and Joshua moved away, leaving Dooley staring after them.

Dooley shook his head. He had no idea what Don wanted but all he himself wanted to do was to find Daci and ensure that she was safe. He walked back to the conference room and was soon immersed in his investigation, forgetting to eat and only rising to refresh his cup of coffee. He was puzzled as to why this had never been solved. It certainly seemed solvable.

Sitting back at last, Dooley frowned at the wall across from him. He had been using the white boards to make his notes. Hearing a noise, he turned to find Toryn sitting beside him.

"Dooley? Heading out soon? You need to." Toryn was worried about his friend, just as he worried about all of his officers.

"I am, Toryn. This case is strange. There is no way that it should not have been solved."

"We understand that. You'll solve it. Head off. But first, before you go, how are you really doing?"

Dooley shrugged once more. He had no idea how he was to feel or what emotions he should expect.

"I don't know, Toryn. I really don't know. I worry so much about Daci. It's not clear which one of us was the target."

"I would suspect Daci. If you had been working on this case at that time, then I would suspect it was you. But no one should know what case that you are working on, outside of the department." Toryn didn't share his thoughts, that an officer was watching Dooley and reporting to whoever it was that was after both Daci and Dooley.

Chapter 17

Two days later, Daci walked through her house. She was afraid for some reason and didn't feel safe in her home. She had no idea why. Stopping in her office, Daci dropped her phone on the desk. She was exhausted, she decided, not sleeping well at night. She had no idea who was behind the assaults and danger that she and Dooley were facing. She ignored the chiming of her phone, choosing instead to walk away from it.

During the night, Daci shot upright in her bed, her heart racing. She listened carefully, thinking that she heard someone in the house. She dressed quietly and then crept through the house, her head moving as she listened carefully. Reaching the living room, Daci hesitated, feeling evil in the room. That had not been the case the night before. She stepped quietly into the room, not reaching for the lights. She knew where everything was in the room.

Hearing a slight noise, Daci began to turn. She didn't make it all the way around to face the man, dressed totally in black, before the bat descended on her head. Daci collapsed without a word, to crumple into a sprawled heap. The man stared down at her before he almost ran from the house, the bat thrown into the bushes. He continued to run up the street, not meeting anyone in the dark.

The next morning, Don approached his sister's home. He wasn't sure even now if she would let him in. He paused as he heard footsteps and turned to find Dooley approaching him, a worried look on his face.

"Don? Have you seen Daci? She's not responding to my calls and she always does." Dooley stared at the front door, a hand going out to stop Don from walking forward. "Her door's open."

Don spun to stare at it. Dooley was correct. The door was open and it shouldn't have been. Daci was not that careless.

Dooley stopped Don from entering the house. He pulled out his weapon to hold it in two hands, walking slowly through the house. He crouched beside Daci for a moment, a hand out to reassure himself that she was alive. Dooley raised himself back to his feet and continued to search for any intruders even as he only wanted to stay beside his lady.

Don looked up as he heard the sounds of sirens breaking through the silent morning air. He frowned and then paled. He almost ran to the front door, meeting Dooley as he was coming back out.

"Daci's hurt, Don, but she's alive. I can't let you in until the teams have been through." He pointed back at Don's car. "Stay there. I'll make sure that you go with her." Dooley turned to the responding officers and sorted out what needed to be done. He watched as the paramedics hurried past him.

Don paced beside his car, his eyes on the house. He had reached out to his parents, who promised to meet him at the hospital. They asked no questions. Even if they had, Don had no answers for them. He turned as he heard the squeak of the stretcher wheels.

—

He was beside the stretcher, his eyes on his sister. Don grimaced at the sight of the bruise on the side of his sister's face.

Daci's parents looked up as Don sat beside his mother. He had no words to say other than that Daci had been attacked in her home.

David and Deree exchanged glances. They had always been afraid of something like this but had prayed that it would never happen.

"Do you know anything, Don?" David watched his son closely.

Don shook his head.

"No, I don't, Dad. I had headed to her home to talk with her. Dooley showed up, saw the open front door, and went through the house. He's the one who found her. He said he'd be here as soon as he could." Don looked up to see Aidan striding through the waiting room. He sighed. This is not how the day was to have gone. And it didn't seem as if it was going to get better any time soon.

Aidan stood in a corner of the examination room, assessing Daci as best as he could. He was frustrated. How had her assailant managed to enter her home? Daci was too careful, he knew, with her security system. He moved forward to the stretcher as the nurse walked away.

Staring down at his friend, Aidan was troubled. He saw the deep bruising on the side of her face. It had been reported to him that a bat had been found outside of her home. They weren't confident, however, that any evidence would be found on it other than from Daci.

Dooley approached him at last, standing beside the stretcher, a hand out to hold one of Daci's. He found her fingers curling around his hand.

"Dooley? Talk to me. I know you've given the brief statement but what was going on there?" Aidan turned to his friend and fellow detective.

"What happened? I'm not sure. It looks as if Daci was awakened in the night, dressed and then headed through her house. She didn't call for help and that worries me. I found her in the living room, unconscious. She hadn't roused by the time that they moved her out and to here." Dooley was frustrated. "I have no idea how the man got into her home." He paled at a thought. "Did he get in there over the evening when she was outside and the back door was unlocked?"

The two men shared a look. That was entirely a possibility. Aidan sighed. This just increased his work and he had enough as it was. He finally walked away, heading out of the hospital through the ambulance bays. He stood for a moment, his face raised to the warm sun, hearing the noise that was inherent in a city hitting his ears. All he could was pray for his friends, and that was enough, he knew. God was in control and had a plan and purpose for what Daci and Dooley were going through.

Daci began to rouse, moaning slightly as her head turned and the injured side of her face hit the pillow. She clung to the hand that was holding hers, thinking that it was a lifeline for her. She had no idea what had happened, but she trusted God enough to know that He had her best in mind. She just didn't have to like it, she decided.

Dooley watched as she roused, knowing that he had to speak with her before she spoke with her parents. He leaned on the bedrail, a slight smile on his face.

"Daci? Are you waking up?" His voice was quiet in the room, yet held the love in it that he felt for her.

"Where am I? And just who are you?" Daci cracked open one eye and stared up at Dooley. "I know you."

"You do. I'm Dooley, and we're dating. Now, what can you tell me about what happened?" Dooley waited patiently for Daci to respond.

"We are? I don't remember that, but if you say that is the case, then I guess it is." Daci reached for the controls to raise the end of the bed. "What happened to me?"

"You were attacked in your own home sometime over night. I doubt that you saw the man. There were no lights on in the house when I entered it." Dooley watched as she finally nodded.

"I don't remember it." Daci looked up at him. "Where's my family?"

"Your family? You remember them?"

"Had I forgotten them?" Daci frowned at him.

"You had, Daci." Dooley quickly recapped that had happened, seeing the horror that crossed her face.

"That happened? I don't remember." Daci was agitated.

Dooley walked away to find her parents and then stood as David and Deree approached their daughter. Daci looked up and then threw herself at her mother, her sobs filling the room.

Don stood beside Dooley, a hand on the other man's shoulder.

"She's remembered?"

"She has, Don, and now has to relive all that over again." Dooley walked away, sorrow in his heart for his lady but prayers heading heavenward for her and her family.

Chapter 18

Don tracked Dooley down that evening. Dooley had wanted to find Daci but with the recovery of her memory, he wasn't sure how to approach her as a friend or even if he should. Don walked into Dooley's backyard, finding Dooley seated on his back deck.

"The coffee's hot, Don. Help yourself." Dooley waved a hand at the door.

Don nodded before he headed into the kitchen and poured himself a mug of coffee. He stared at it, thinking that was all he was doing lately, drinking coffee and getting nowhere in the investigation.

Back outside, Don sat quietly, not saying anything. Dooley appreciated that, but he was still puzzled by the event at Daci's home. He had spoken with Aidan who could give him very little more information than he already had.

"Don? Have you spoken with Daci?" Dooley finally broke the silence between them.

"Not since this morning. She went home, I do know that. She's refused to let Mom and Dad go with her. She's gone into protective mode." Don was frustrated at that.

"She will. It's innate in her, I think. She was doing that when she lost her memory. She buried whatever it was deep inside and didn't want to remember. She's afraid for you and your parents."

—

"She is. I got that from how she reacted earlier. She just walked out of the hospital, leaving us standing and staring after her." Don gave a small grin at the remembered way that Daci had stomped away from them.

"She would do that." Dooley had sent a text off to Daci which she had responded to, simply telling him that they would talk on the next day and that she was heading for bed. He read between the lines and knew that she was afraid to be alone. She would just refuse to have anyone with her.

"What can you tell me, Dooley? What happened?" Don was grasping at straws.

"Not a lot, Don. Not a lot. Aidan is really the one who you need to speak with. I can tell that she was unconscious when I found her as you know. I don't know if there was any evidence recovered or not." Dooley would not say what he had been told.

"I have talked to him." Don sighed. "He can't say much."

"No, he can't." Dooley sighed, exhausted from the emotions that were roiling through him.

Don stayed for a while longer, praying with his friend. He knew that it would only get worse for Dooley and Daci.

Dooley walked into the conference room the next day, not wanting to be there but knowing that he had to continue working on the case. He frowned as he walked towards the white boards, reading the information that he written there. He was missing an important piece of information that was needed to solve it.

He turned as he heard a soft tap at the door and opened it. He reached for Daci, drawing her into the room and simply wrapping her into his arms. His prayer whispered down to her ears.

Daci leaned into Dooley, feeling safe again. She didn't want to move from him but she did. She walked through the room, reading his notes, not sure if she should be doing that.

Dooley leaned against a table, watching her. He knew that he should stop her but he didn't. He needed her input on what he had found.

"Dooley? What are you trying to find here?" Daci tapped at the board that held the Evans' demographics.

"What was I trying to find? I'm not sure. I was just listing everything that I could find. I'm not familiar with them." Dooley walked over to her, wrapping an arm around her. He felt her leaning against him.

"I was with the younger ones. They were always in trouble in school." Daci bit at her lip. "Dooley? With my memory coming back, does this change anything?" She was hesitant to ask him.

"Change anything? You mean, us as a couple?" At her nod, he simply kissed her cheek. "That changes nothing. I'm glad that you do remember. It was stressing you out that you couldn't or wouldn't."

She frowned at him. He had worded it the same way that Don had that morning.

"Why would you state it that way, that I wouldn't remember?"

"Because our minds do strange things when we're injured or in danger. You did that." Dooley hesitated for a moment. "I prayed that you would remember. I just didn't know if you would or if you would still want to be friends with me."

"I wouldn't do that, Dooley. You're too important to me. We love each other, don't we?" Daci felt as if she was begging him.

"I would never walk away from you, Daci. I love you and want to keep you safe. I just don't know how to do that." Dooley hugged her and then turned back to the board. "What can you tell me about the younger ones?"

Daci reached for a pad of paper and pen, finding a seat at the table to work away. Dooley watched her and then walked back to where he had the folders. He sat and was soon engrossed in what he was studying. He was on his feet an hour later, heading for the white boards to add material to it.

Daci looked up at that point, studying Dooley. She could only thank God that Dooley was in her life and that he was a strong Christian.

Dooley turned back to Daci, reaching for her papers. He read through them before he nodded.

"This is great, Daci. You've added information and details that I don't have." He hugged her and then walked with her to the outside. "You need to be doing something."

"I do. I need to find the shelter and the employees. I owe them a big apology." Daci wasn't sure how to proceed in that.

"You don't. They understand what you went through and hold no grudges." Dooley kissed her and then closed the car door after her. He didn't want her to drive away but knew that they both had work to do. "Let's go out for a meal tonight, love."

"I would like that. Come and find me when you're done. I'll be at home." Daci refused to walk away from her home. God was her strength in what she was facing. She had acknowledged her weakness and fear to Him and spent hours before Him until she had the peace that only came from HIm.

Dooley watched her drive away before he walked towards Ben's diner. He needed some time to think away from the office. He had too much information whirling around in his mind.

Ben nodded at him, pointing towards his office. He followed Dooley that way, handing over a meal that he had grabbed for Dooley.

"Dooley? You're troubled?" Ben waited for Dooley to look up at him.

"I am, Ben. I really am. I'm still working on that case and Daci has given me more information." He nodded at the look on Ben's face. "She was assaulted last night in her home. That assault triggered her memory again. She's hurting in more ways than one."

"She will be. All you can do is to be there and hold her when you can. Pray for her. Support her decisions." Ben grinned. "You could always marry her, Dooley. You're both ready for that.

Chapter 19

Dooley walked towards Daci that evening as she stood outside of Ben's diner. This is not how he had planned to meet her. He had been late leaving his work, involved in a phone call that could have waited but he chose to take it. It had proven to be beneficial.

Daci walked into his hug, feeling cherished and safe once more. She looked up at him, seeing the stress in his eyes.

"Dooley? Are you okay?" Daci was worried about him.

"I'm okay, Daci. Just troubled about something that I have to leave with God. As a human, we want to solve whatever it is right away. We forget that it is in His timing and in His plans." He stared down at the beautiful face looking up at him before he kissed her.

"That is so true, Dooley. We do want to solve it by ourselves." Daci reached for the hand that he was extending. "You're hungry." She smirked at him.

"And so are you. Let's see what Ben can come up with for us." He held the door for her, not seeing the two men who followed them into the diner and then chose a table where they could watch the couple.

Ben's wife, Rachel, approached the couple, a huge smile on her face. She had scoffed at Ben when he said that Dooley and Daci were a couple, but she could not scoff any more. The evidence was right in front of her, in person.

Daci looked up at Rachel and greeted her before her eyes turned to the table where the two men were sitting. She was afraid suddenly, just holding back the shudders that shook her body. She sensed that Dooley was watching her and she shook her head at him.

Later that evening, Dooley was troubled. Daci had not volunteered what had bothered her at the diner. He had taken a look around, seeing the table that was in her line of sight. He mentally memorized the descriptions of them. He had taken the time to write them down once he had returned home. Daci had simply told him that she would be at the shelter the next day. Dooley had nodded, knowing that he had to concentrate as well on his own investigation. Only that investigation seemed to be drawing in the women's shelter and that troubled him.

Finding his prayer corner, Dooley could do nothing more than sit in silence before his Heavenly Father. He needed to find the peace that He alone could give and that he desperately needed. He waited patiently for hours before he rose, peace once more in his heart. He had fought it out with God about being in control and taking care of Daci.

Daci walked into the new women's shelter the next morning. She felt uncomfortable being there, knowing that she had to be but only wanting to be where Dooley was. She was afraid for him, afraid more than she was for herself. She had had a long talk with Don the night before, apologizing over and over for not remembering him. He had given a soft laugh and said that it was okay and that she had done that to protect herself and likely protect everyone else in her life. He had prayed for her and then asked if she could meet with Don and his team sometime over the next day or so. She had agreed, just asking if Dooley could be there. This affected him as much as it did her. Don had been quiet for a moment, thinking through his sister's relationship with the detective, before he had readily agreed.

Looking around her office, Daci sighed. She had so much to catch up on, she knew, but she would catch up on her work. Her purse was locked into a drawer as she sat behind her desk. Her computer was booted up as she looked through the folders that sat on the desk. Daci was pleasantly surprised. The work had been kept as up to date as she would. There was very little that she was behind in. She raised a prayer of thanks for those who worked with her.

Daci was on her feet two hours later to walk through a building that she was not familiar with. She greeted the residents, seeing new faces among them. She would need to learn their stories. Finally, the end of the day came, and she was free to leave. Daci hesitated to walk out of the building until she saw Paul and Joshua waiting for her.

"What are you two doing here?" She frowned as they grinned at her. "Don sent you, didn't he?"

"He did." Paul reached for her keys. "Let me go over your car, Daci. It's been sitting here all day, has it not?"

Daci nodded even as she heard Joshua chuckling beside her.

"You think this is funny!" Daci's accusation made Joshua laugh even harder.

"It is, in a way. This is what we all went through, you know." Joshua shot her a smirk as he said that.

"Yes, you did. I didn't plan on this, you know."

"None of us did. God saw us through. He's with you, Daci. You know that. You've heard all the promises and prayers. You've said more than a few yourself. We can't tell you how to react or when to run or when to stand and fight. That is a decision that you make, you and God. And of course, Dooley. He's not walking away from you. Not at all." Joshua reached to hug the lady who he considered a sister. "We're praying for you, Daci. We don't want to see you or Dooley hurt worse than you have been."

Paul handed her back her keys before he walked to the passenger's side of the vehicle. Daci glared at him for a moment before she sighed.

"Obviously, I'm not driving home by myself. Get in, Paul. I want to go home." Daci was resigned that the team was now hovering over her.

"Off we go then. And we are walking through your home before you go in." Paul was adamant about that. They were still puzzled about how the man had gotten in. Caleb had suggested that he was in the basement before Daci had locked up that night. That statement had frightened them all. They all had to admit that was a distinct possibility.

Daci waited patiently for Joshua and Paul to walk through her home and then around the house and yard. Paul walked back towards her, dropping her keys into her outstretched hand.

"All clear, Daci, as far as we can see. There are no secret hiding places here, are there?" Paul said this in jest.

"Hiding places? As in secret?" Daci paled. She had forgotten that there were. She ran for her house, ignoring Paul's shout at her before she heard his footsteps after her, his voice calling for Joshua.

"Daci?" Paul reached out to pull her to a stop. "Where are you going?"

"The spare bedroom. There's a hatch in the closet ceiling. It leads to the attic. I had forgotten about it as I usually use the one in the laundry room."

Joshua headed for the basement for a ladder. He set it up and was climbing it and searching for the catch that would open it. He shoved it up and reached for a flashlight. Joshua heaved himself into the attic, surprised to find that it was finished. He reached for the light switch, seeing how light it was.

"This is big, you know, Daci."

"I know it is. I had completely forgotten it." Daci climbed the ladder high enough to look into the room. "Have you found anything yet?"

Paul had been moving around the room, pausing as he found another hatch.

"There's another hatch here, Daci. It's on the wall. Paul? Can you head out to the back of the house and look for a hatch opening?" Joshua heard Paul's call in response and then his footsteps heading outside.

Joshua pushed against the hatch and found Paul staring up at him. "It comes out just above your back porch, Daci. Did you know that?"

"I most certainly did not." Daci scrambled down from the ladder and ran for the outside. Her hand landed on Paul's back as she stared up at Joshua.

"How hard would it be to open from the outside?"

Joshua had been examining the hatch before he stared at the porch roof. There were scrapes there that weren't from nature.

"Daci? It's easy to open from the outside. Someone has been up here. I would suspect it was the man who assaulted you." Joshua sighed. "We need to call Aidan."

"And Dooley." Daci grumbled at that. "He'll want to see this."

Chapter 20

Carefully approaching Daci, Dooley wrapped his arms around her and drew her back against him. He had not been prepared for her call or the news of what they had found. He shared a look with both Paul and Joshua who shook their heads. None of them had expected this. But it did explain how the man had managed to get into Daci's house. The question they all had was who had known about the hatch and who had been that man.

Daci shrugged away from Dooley and walked towards Aidan. She could tell that he was not happy and somewhat angry. She was not happy herself. Someone had been able to access her house without her knowledge.

"Daci? How could you forget that?" Aidan's words spit at he.

"Aidan? Don't yell at me. I really did forget about it. It isn't something that I use. Have you never forgotten anything?" Daci stalked away from him, leaving him staring after her.

Don approached him, Delanie with him. He shook his head. He knew that at some point, Daci and Aidan would butt heads and that just happened.

"Aidan? Daci giving you a hard time?" Don grinned at him.

"She is. Did you know that she had a hidden room in her attic?" Aidan was frustrated.

"I did, now that you mention it. I had forgotten it as well. That's how the man got in?" Don was angry at his forgetfulness.

"It is. We need to block it so that never happens again." Aidan walked away, heading for the crime scene tech who was approaching him.

Don shook his head before he headed for where he saw Dooley standing with Daci. Paul and Joshua had left, promising that they would be back in the morning.

"Daci?" Don's quiet voice had Daci staring at him. She looked past him to see their parents approaching.

"Who called Mom and Dad?" Daci was frustrated at that. She had planned a quiet evening at home. That plan had walked out the door long ago.

"I have no idea. Perhaps Aidan did." Don hugged his mother and then watched as his parents hugged his sister. He smiled to himself as she moved back from them and towards Dooley, who willingly wrapped her into his arms.

"They're in love, Don." Delanie kept her voice low, knowing that only he could hear her.

"They are. That they are. We just need to solve this and then they can move on with their lives." Don watched Delanie's face. "Delanie?"

"They may not wait for then, Don. Some of us didn't. You know that."

"I do. And if they do, then we support them no matter what our feelings are." Don moved towards the house, following Daci and Dooley and their parents.

Aidan was waiting for Daci, a hand out to stop her from moving past him.

"I'm sorry, Daci. I should not have spoken in a harsh tone with you. But I am worried and frustrated. We are not getting anywhere with your case and we should be."

"Thank you for the apology, Aidan. I understand your frustration. It is the same that you felt with Don and his team. We can't change what has happened nor can we move forward without being in danger. God is in control. He has already determined the path that we walk. He has gone before us on it and will allow nothing that is not in His will for us." Daci looked up at Aidan, feeling Dooley's chin against her head as he nodded in agreement.

"I understand that, Daci. I've been there. I just worry about you." Aidan looked around. "How do we keep you safe, though?"

"It's not up to you, Aidan. It's up to God. Both Dooley and I accept that. We go on with our lives and trust that He will be with us. If His will means that we graduate to heaven, then we do. The ones left behind will grieve but God will be their comfort." Daci moved past Aidan, speaking with the crime scene tech who was leaving.

Dooley watched her. She had come to a conclusion that he was still struggling with. It didn't mean that she was that much further ahead in her walk with God. It just meant that they were coming to that conclusion in their own time and with God's leading. He walked after her, leaving Don, Delanie, David, and Deree staring after them and then staring at Aidan.

"Aidan?" Don's voice finally broke through the silence, a silence that seemed deafening.

"Don? How did she forget that room?" Aidan was still struggling to understand that.

"I think that she was up there when she bought the house and had no reason to go up there after that. It's one of those things that slip our mind. She had no reason to remember it." David spoke up. He too had forgotten about that room.

"I see. We've blocked it from the inside now so that no one can enter from the outside." Aidan walked away, needing to be elsewhere. He was unhappy with how he had to leave the investigation but he had no choice.

Deree searched for her daughter, finding her in the kitchen working at getting a meal for them all. She just hugged her daughter once more and worked to help to prepare the meal. The two ladies could hear the quiet conversation of the men before Delanie joined them.

"Daci?" Delanie's quiet voice reached through Daci's dark thoughts. "How can we help you?"

Daci shrugged. She was a victim of crime and needed help. She just didn't know how to ask for it or what to ask for.

"I don't know, Delanie. I really don't know. If it were one of my ladies, I would know what to ask for or what to say." She blinked, overcome by tears for a moment before she swallowed hard and sent her emotions back into herself.

"So, then, what would you tell them? I'm sure that it's similar to what you told me and all the other ladies who you have helped." Delanie waited patiently for Daci to control her emotions and then respond.

Deree watched the two younger women, thanking God for Delanie. She was just who Daci needed to speak with. She had been through danger with Don and could understand to a certain degree just what Daci and Dooley were facing. Deree could not, not that she didn't want to. She had just not faced what both her son and daughter had faced.

Daci kept working on the meal, not responding to Delanie's question. Her thoughts were troubled, she had to admit, and had to turn those troubled thoughts and doubts over to God. She looked up at Delanie, to find her sister-in-law watching her. She gave a small smile.

"I don't know exactly what I would say to them. I would just tell them that God loves them and cares about them. That He doesn't want harm to come to them but sometimes He allows danger and harm and hurt to us. We have no idea what His plans for us are or what purpose He has for what we go through. I would pray with them and then leave them to ponder on the thoughts."

Delanie was nodding. She agreed with what Daci had said. She could see Deree listening and then understanding what Daci was saying. She looked up to see Dooley watching from just outside of the kitchen, his eyes on his lady. She frowned for a moment before she reached to hug Daci. Picking up a tray of food, she walked away as did Deree.

Dooley walked towards his lady and found that she was turning to him. He wrapped her into his arms, sorrow in his heart that she was facing this. He wanted to end the mystery and bring her through to safety. He just couldn't do that.

"Okay, love?" His voice was only audible to her.

Daci shrugged for a moment before she sighed.

"I don't know, Dooley. I just don't know. I'm scared to be on my own but I can't go to anyone else's and bring danger to them."

"Marry me, Daci. Marry me. I'll keep you safe." Dooley's words were whispered in her ear.

Daci stiffened for a moment and then relaxed against him. She appreciated Dooley's words and the reason for them. They just weren't ready for that step, not yet. It might come to that but now was not the time for them to marry.

"Thank you, Dooley. I'll pray about it but we're not ready for this. Not yet." Daci felt Dooley's arms tighten around her as he prayed for them.

Chapter 21

Three days later, Dooley was on the move once more. He had tracked down a member of the Evans family who had agreed to speak with him. That woman had appeared in the lobby of the police department, asking for him. Somehow, word had reached the streets that he was working on that cold case. Dooley had no idea who had spoken, almost out of turn, but he was grateful.

He studied the woman before he walked forward and greeted her. He knew her. Ella Evans had been active in the community until she had retired from her teaching career.

"Mrs. Evans?" Dooley spoke from beside her, startling her. "Come with me." He handed her a visitor's badge and then led her to one of the interrogation rooms. "Have a seat. Can I get you anything?"

"Some water would be nice. Thank you, young man." Ella watched as Dooley walked away to return with two bottles of water and then sat across from her. "I hope that I am not wasting your time, young man, but I heard that you were working on the Evans murder."

"I could be. You're here. What can you tell me about the Evans' family?" Dooley reached for his pen, watching her intently as she hesitated for a moment. "Mrs. Evans?"

"It's Miss Evans. I never married. Let me speak and then you can ask what you need to clarify." Ella Evans did just that, telling the history of the Evans' family and what crimes they had been involved in.

Dooley made his notes, watching her intently if she hesitated at all.

"Miss Evans? You mention that the man who was murdered? He was not involved in crime?"

"No, Joe was never involved in crime. He tried to stay on the straight and narrow as they say. He was distraught at the crimes that were being committed in our family name. He was my older brother. As I said, I had two other brothers. They are the ones who were involved in crime. My suspicion has always been that he was killed as a threat towards John and Jerry. I don't know for sure. There was no evidence found, not that I am aware of."

Dooley gave a sad smile. There was evidence. It had just been left in the boxes, not investigated at all. He had changed that. The crime scene tech assigned to help him had been dismayed that the evidence had sat there all those years. He would make it a priority, he reassured Dooley.

"There is evidence, Miss Evans. I'm working on that now. I pray that I can solve this for you and bring whoever it was who killed your brother to justice." He rose at last, helping her to her feet and then tucking her hand into the crook of his arm. Dooley watched as she walked away from him before he looked up. "God, this would be a good time for You to step in. I am afraid of what and who I'll discover. And I fear for my lady. They seem to think that she knows something but she says that she doesn't. I'll need to speak with her again about the house."

Daci turned from her office in the shelter building late that afternoon. She greeted the ladies and children as she walked through the building, heading for her car. Daci paused as she saw Don waiting for her. She sighed. What was happening now? She was tired of this.

"Don? What's happened now?" Daci stopped short of where he was standing, hands jammed into a jean jacket pockets.

"Nothing, sis. I just wanted to spend some time with you. Are you meeting Dooley for a meal?" Don reached to hug his sister, worried more than he could express.

"No, he's working late, he said. You want a meal together? We haven't done that in a while, just the two of us." Daci hugged him back.

"No, we haven't and we need to do that. Delanie is at a meeting and threw me out for the evening. She sent me to spend the time with you." Don grinned as he remembered how Delanie had shoved him out of the door and then locked it behind him, a smirk on her face.

"She did, did she?" Daci linked her arm with her brother. "Where's your truck?"

"Mark dropped me off. I was hoping to catch a ride home with you, if that works." Don grinned down at his sister.

"We can do that." Daci pulled back a chair at a table in the local fish and chips shop. "I've been hungry for fish and chips. Davy does the best in town."

"He does. And we haven't been here in a while." Don nodded at their server, knowing that they would receive what they usually ordered. It was just how it worked in that shop. "How are you really doing, sis?"

Daci looked down at the hands that she had clasped together on the tabletop. She really didn't know how to answer that.

"I'm not sure, Don. I really am not." She looked up at her brother, blinking rapidly to dispel the tears that clouded her vision. "You know how it is. You've been through it."

"I have, but each adventure is different. I worry about you, Daci." Don reached out a hand to lay it on her hands. "I know that you're struggling with your faith. It happens. God will never leave you, you understand that. He covers you with His hand. He has walked this path before you. I can't tel you how to react or how to act. That's between you and God. Stay close to Dooley. He's moving in and taking over your protection and security. It's okay. I know that at some point, I'll have to step back as will the others. They worry about you, Daci, but understand that you don't want any harm to come to them."

"I know that they do, Don. They have done that since you set up your team. I have Dooley in my life now. He's not walking away from me." She gave a small smile as he stared at her. "We're talking, Don. That's all I will say."

———

"Fair enough. Now, what about the shelter? Is it running okay still? What do you need for it?" Don had reached out to a friend of theirs, Barnabas Carey from The Barnabas Foundation. "Barnabas is weighing in. He's talked to their board and they are forwarding funds to do whatever it is that you need to set back up properly." Don knew that the funds and assistant available came without any strings attached.

"He is? That's wonderful. I'll talk to him or Breck. They've been through so much as well." Daci rose at last, unable to eat any more. "I need to get home, Don."

"That you do." He hugged his sister after they had walked out of the restaurant. "Delanie's here. We'll follow you home."

———

Chapter 22

Frustrated, Dooley threw his pen on the table and then hid his face in his hands. He was at a standstill for this case and that troubled him to no degree. He wanted to solve it, having the idea that if he were able to solve it, he would solve the adventure that he and Daci were involved in. Dooley rose at last, pacing the room, studying the white boards. He sighed once more, something he felt that he was doing too much.

Dooley turned as he heard a tap and the door and then the door opened. Toryn and Lyle walked in, bags of food in their hands. Dooley glanced at the clock and signed once more. He had forgotten to eat once more.

"Let's eat, Dooley. Then we can pray with you. Then you tell us what's got you so frustrated." Lyle grinned at him. "I know you're not on my squad any more but you're still my friend and as such we need to keep you in our prayers."

"Thanks, fellows. This means a lot. And yes, I am frustrated." Dooley reached for the bag with his burger and fries. "This is good."

"It is." Toryn finally sat back, their prayer time finished. "What are you frustrated with on this case, Dooley?"

Dooley snorted, bringing smiles to the men's faces.

"That I can't solve it yesterday." Dooley wiped at his mouth with the paper napkin. He crumbled the napkin before he looked at the two men with him. "I just need that one piece of information to solve it and at this point, I'm not sure that we will ever find it."

Lyle was on his feet, reading the white boards. He nodded. Dooley had written his information and thoughts in a concise and orderly manner. Lyle paused at the last one, reading the brief notes from the interview with Ella Evans.

"Dooley? You've met with Ella Evans?" Lyle turned to watch Dooley.

"I did. She didn't give much more information than we had." Dooley watched Lyle carefully. "Do you know her?"

"I do. She lived in our neighbourhood for a number of years. She kept to herself, not really interacting with anyone. She moved a few years ago, to a senior's apartment if I remember correctly."

"I see. She didn't say that." Dooley sat back for a moment before he reached for his notes. Toryn reached for them to read through them.

"Dooley? Where were you heading with these thoughts?" Toryn pointed to Dooley's notes midway down the page.

Dooley shrugged. He wasn't sure what Toryn meant but he didn't know what he was looking for and stated that.

That afternoon, Daci trudged towards her home. She was exhausted, not sleeping well lately. She looked up as she felt someone near her. Daci's face lit up. Dooley was sitting on her front steps and waiting for her, a huge smile on his face.

———

Dooley was on his feet, wrapping Daci into a hug. He suddenly wanted to marry her and not let her leave him at all. He just felt that it was too soon. Daci had claimed his heart and he would give it to no one else.

"Daci? You're home." He leaned back to look down at her face, frowning for a moment. "You are exhausted."

"I am. The stress of working and worrying about keeping everybody safe is taking its toll. I told the board that I was stepping down for now. I can't put anyone at risk." Daci blinked back her tears. Her emotions were raw. She loved her work but also didn't want anyone hurt because of her.

"I see. Okay. That's a good decision, I guess. You'll have prayed over it." Dooley had no doubt that she had. "And also sought counsel."

"I have. I just can't do this, Dooley." She leaned against him, her defeat evident to him. "Going through what the guys did and what Don did? That's worn me down." Daci yawned, feeling safe enough with Dooley to let her barriers down. "Dooley? Marry me?" Daci slept, not seeing the soft smile that lit Dooley's face.

"I will, Daci. In a heartbeat." He swept her into his arms and carried her back to his truck. He headed for her parents' place.

David looked askance as Dooley carried Daci towards the house.

"Dooley?" David reached to rest a hand on his daughter's hair. "What happened?"

"Her physical strength just gave out. She's overwrought and discouraged. She also has taken a leave from her work." Dooley watched carefully as he entered the house, heading for the living room and laid her gently on the couch.

Deree moved into to cover her daughter before she reached to hug Dooley, turning him back towards the kitchen. It was mealtime but none of them really felt like eating.

"Dooley? You brought Daci here?" Deree watched the younger man carefully, knowing that he was deeply concerned about Daci.

"I did. I was talking with her and she just fell asleep. I couldn't go into her home so I brought her here." Dooley bit at his lip, uncertain if he had done the right thing. He didn't have to work for the next week, forced to take the time off. "I just brought her to her parents."

"You did the right thing, son." David laid a hand on Dooley's shoulder before he shoved him down onto a chair. "She'll sleep for a while." He grinned at Dooley. "And you are not going anywhere, that much we know."

Dooley nodded. He would not walk away from Daci, not then, not ever. She was the one who he had been waiting for, the one who completed him.

Dooley grinned for a moment, causing Deree to ask him what was funny.

"Daci asked me to marry her just as she was falling asleep." Dooley continued to grin, his thoughts on the moment. "Has she ever done anything like that before?"

Deree and David shared a look.

"She's never done that before, Dooley." David thought through it and nodded. "She trusts you in a way that she doesn't trust anyone else, Dooley, not even her family. You make her feel safe and cherished. And that's how it should be."

Dooley sat back at that, acknowledging David's words before he rose and paced into the living room where he sat on the floor, an arm across Daci. His head bent as he began to pray for his lady.

———

Chapter 23

Daci roused a couple of hours later, staring around. She had no idea how she had managed to make it to her parents' home. She had no memory of driving there. Daci stared at Dooley, who still sat in front of the couch on the floor, a Bible open on his knees.

Dooley looked around as he felt Daci moving. He smiled at her, worried as well.

"Daci? You're awake." Dooley moved to let Daci sit up and then sat beside her, an arm wrapped around her.

"I am. How did I get here?"

"You fell sleep on your feet. I brought you here." Dooley watched her carefully. "You also said that you were taking a leave of absence from your work."

"I did. I can't put them at risk." Daci leaned against Dooley.

"No, you can't." Dooley stretched out his legs, crossing his ankles. "I'm off for the next week."

"You are?" Daci's face lit up at that. "But what about that cold case?"

"It's there. I'll pick it up again when I go back in a week. I'm at an impasse right at the moment." Dooley yawned himself. "I need to head for home, Daci. Stay here for the night. I'll stop by in the morning." He kissed her and then walked away, the front door closing quietly after him.

Daci was on her feet and out on the front porch, watching as he left, suddenly feeling bereft. She felt her mother's arm around her.

"Daci?" Deree waited for her daughter to respond.

"Mom? How do I do this? How do I stay safe and make sure that Dooley stays safe as well? I know. I know. He's a police officer and knows what to watch for. Don has trained me well as well." Daci looked at her mother, seeing the concern on Deree's face.

"I can tell you what I would do. That's not necessarily what you could do. Talk with Don and his team again. Talk to their ladies, Shanli, Artis, Keller. You can reach out to Abe and his team and Richard and his team. You have resources that you have accumulated through your work."

"I know, Mom. It just doesn't make it any easier, does it?" Daci grew even more sober. "I worry about Dooley. I'm afraid that he will be seriously hurt or killed because of me."

Deree watched her daughter before she drew her back into the house. David shut and locked the door behind him before he followed his ladies to the sunroom. He sat in his favourite chair, his eyes on his daughter, his heart praying for her.

"It is a choice that is his to make. He has made it obvious that you are the light and love of his life. I suspect that he is yours." Deree's hand rested on

Daci's. "He needs to hear that from you before anyone else does. I suspect that you are close to coming to an agreement." She laughed for a moment. "Dooley said that you asked him to marry you just as you fell asleep."

"I did? I've never done that before." Daci was horrified at what her mother had said.

"You trust him, Daci, in a way that you don't trust anyone else, including us. He makes you feel safe, cherished, and loved. It is out there for all of us to see. And you react the same with him. He has your heart, Daci. We can all see that."

Daci sighed, startled to see her father sitting there. David simply sent her a father's smile and then began to pray for the couple.

Dooley stepped back from his door just after he had arrived home. Aidan and Kaelen, another close friend, stepped inside. He looked down at the sandwich he was holding in his hand and sighed. So much for his supper, he decided.

"Fellows? Are you here for a reason or just because?" He grinned at them, finding them grinning back at him.

"Just because." Kaelen walked past him, heading for the coffee pot. "How old is the coffee?"

"Not that old. I just got home from Daci's parents about thirty minutes ago." Dooley sank into his chair, his sandwich back on his plate.

Kaelen shared a look with Aidan before he set their mugs of coffee on the table. He watched Dooley carefully, seeing how close to the edge he was.

"Dooley? What can you tell us? I fly helicopters but I did go through something with Keller."

"Not a lot, Kaelen. I really don't know what I can say." Dooley studied the plate that held his sandwich before he shoved it to one side. "There is just something missing, and I don't know what it is."

Aidan had had a long conversation with both John and Lyle. He was freeing up time to work with Dooley once he was back from his enforced vacation.

"I'm planning on working with you when you go back next week, Dooley. John and Lyle have agreed to that. We'll work together to see what we have. I'll go over what you've done before then." Aidan studied Dooley. "How's Daci?"

"She burnt out. She stepped back from her work for now, and that hurts her heart." Dooley was worried for her. "Daci is hurting in so many ways. She understands only too well what can happen."

"She does." Aidan paused, not sure how to continue. "Dooley? Have you thought about marrying her?"

Dooley nodded. He had thought of that, and a small smile crossed his face as he remembered how Daci had proposed to him.

"I have thought of that. We're not ready for that step. I don't know that we will ever be. We need to solve this first. And that I don't know how to do."

Dooley's head dropped for a moment even as he heard
his friends praying for him.

Chapter 24

Daci paced through her home the next day, anger sparking from her. She had arrived home to find her home spray painted with threats. Aidan had been around as had the crime scene techs. She no longer felt safe in her home. Daci could hear Dooley's voice floating in from the outdoors as he spoke with Aidan and then Don. She sighed. Of course, Don would appear. She just prayed the rest of the team had not shown up. That was not the case, she saw. Joshua and Caleb had appeared in her line of sight, walking through her home to tighten up the security of her home.

Dooley walked towards Daci, simply wrapping her in his arms. His chin rested on the top of her head. He didn't say anything. He didn't feel the need to.

Daci struggled to turn in Dooley's arms and hugged him in return. She didn't see the speculative looks sent their way.

Don approached them, a smile on his face as he watched his sister.

"Dooley? You're off this week?"

"I am. Why?"

"Because that means you and Daci can spend the week together, being out there, and maybe end this." Don gave them what advice he could, knowing full well that he was preaching at the choir as the saying goes.

"We realize that, Don." Dooley was deep in thought. He had no idea how to proceed at this point, wanting it over and over now.

"We know that you understand all this, Dooley. It's what we do, you understand that. We will be there when we can. We won't intrude but we will do what we can to protect you both." Don finally left, his team leaving with him.

Daci pushed away from Dooley, walking back through her home. It was not disturbed, not on the inside. She would need to paint the garage doors but that would be a task for the next day. She worried about her neighbours but wasn't convinced that they were at risk from anyone.

Dooley watched her patiently, knowing that she had to digest what had happened and think through the ramifications of what was happening and would happen. He sighed. This was not how it was supposed to be.

Daci moved back towards Dooley, walking into his hug. She sighed to herself. She didn't want Dooley to leave but he had to.

"Dooley? How do we go on?" Daci didn't really expect him to answer.

"We pray it through, love. We pray it through. And then we make plans. For now, come and lock up after me. Aidan has promised that patrol vehicles will be around over night and into the morning."

Daci turned back to Dooley, a shuttered look on her face. She was terrified, she had to admit.

———

"Dooley? What can we do today? I don't want to stay here." Daci wrapped her arms around her waist, not looking away from him.

Dooley studied her and then shrugged. His hand reached for hers.

"Let's go find some breakfast. Neither of us have eaten, I don't think." Dooley watched as she carefully locked up her home and then tucked her into his truck. "Where would you like to eat?"

"I'm not sure." Daci looked at Dooley and then past him. "Can we leave town?"

"We can. I know of a little diner just outside of town. I go there when I can. It's a mom and pop diner." Dooley drove away, heading out of Oak City and down the highway towards Elmton. Fifteen minutes later, Dooley was pulling into a parking lot at a railway car diner.

Daci stared at it. She had not realized that it was a restaurant. She had passed it many times over the years.

Dooley led her inside, waving at the owners. He was a frequent customer enough that he knew their names and their history.

"Daci? Pick what you want to eat. Everything is delicious." Dooley grinned at her.

Two hours later, Dooley captured Daci's hand in his as they walked towards his truck. His footsteps slowed before they stopped completely. Daci looked up at Dooley before she looked at his truck. Shock covered her face.

"Dooley? Your truck?" Daci could barely get the words out.

"Yeah. My truck. All the tires are flat by the looks of it." Dooley walked around the truck, Daci keeping pace with him. "Someone followed us, I guess." Dooley paused before he pulled out his phone. This was deliberate, he knew.

The patrol officer walked back towards Dooley, who stood with his arms crossed across his chest.

"Dooley? Who'd you anger that much?" The officer pointed back at his truck. "It's not just the tires. Your brake lines are slashed and the exhaust system is damaged."

Dooley merely nodded. He had suspected the brakes.

"I have no idea, George. I have no idea. All I did was step in with Daci and try to protect her." Dooley gave a brief recap of what had been happening.

The officer nodded, turning as he heard the heavy diesel motor of the tow truck. Dooley walked towards the driver and exchanged a few words with him. He turned then and beckoned at Daci, who almost ran towards him. He helped her up into the tow truck cab before jumping up himself.

Back at his home, Dooley was frustrated more than he had ever been. His truck was in a garage for repairs, damage done almost under his eyes. He had taken a seat where he could watch his truck and had seen nothing. All he could do was pray for the situation and for his lady.

Daci found her prayer corner, her head bowed as she prayed for her guy. That was how she now looked at Dooley. She had no idea if he really would be but that didn't stop her prayers for him.

Late that night, dark figures haunted the outside of the houses. They could not find a way in, however. That drew angry words from them before they slunk away, to come back and try again another day or night.

Chapter 25

Aidan dropped his briefcase beside his office desk before he was off to find Lyle. He had spent the day in court and while that case was over, there were many waiting for him.

"Lyle? Where does it stand with Dooley and Daci? I haven't had an update in a couple of days."

Lyle turned to face him, shaking his head.

"No update, Aidan. Just no update. They're out and about with one another. Are they a couple?" Lyle had been puzzled at that.

"They are, I suspect. Dooley doesn't do this and neither does Daci. If they're out there, they have either decided to pretend to be a couple to end it or really are a couple. I would suspect the latter."

Lyle paced the break room, worried about his friend and fellow detective.

"So, if they are pretending, they are doing a very good job of it. Dooley has never dated, never shown an interest in any lady until Daci. And Daci, while she collects friends, has never dated either. This is strange for them."

"It is strange, Lyle, but if they are a true couple, we'll find out shortly I would suspect." Aidan didn't know how to phrase what he wanted to know. "Do you know where the case stands with the Evans case?"

"No, I don't. John isn't saying much, just tells me to speak with Dooley. You're working with him next week, correct?" Lyle eyed Aidan, praying that they were not overwhelming him.

"I am. I'm going to spend tomorrow going over what he's found and see what conclusions I come to. It may mean a lot of legwork on our part, re-interviewing the witnesses and family, those who are still around."

"It's been what twenty years or so? You both would have been young at that time."

"We were. I can still remember reading and hearing about the murder. It has always intrigued me that it was never solved at that point." Dooley stared at the tiled floor for a moment before he looked up. "Who sold out?"

Lyle nodded. He and Dooley had discussed that very fact.

"That's what we think, Aidan. Someone sold out to the Evans or whoever it was that did the murder. I pray that we can determine who it was but the chances are low." Lyle was frustrated at that.

"It is tough. Let me talk with Dooley and see what he has come up with. He may have some ideas." Aidan walked away, heading back for his office. He had work to do. He just didn't feel doing it and that was a problem.

Dooley turned back from his door that night. Aidan had shown up and from the look on his face, he meant to have a long conversation with Dooley.

"Have a seat, Aidan. And then tell me what's on your mind." Dooley sat, his facial expression not changing from the shuttered one he had assumed when he saw Aidan.

"I will do that, Dooley. First, we need to pray. You need that and so does Daci." Aidan was as good as his words and prayed for his friends. He looked up at Dooley at that point. "Dooley. Talk to me about the Evans case. I'm heading in there again tomorrow to go over your notes. What should I be looking for?"

"I really don't know, Aidan. I really don't. That case has been mishandled since the start and then just left on the shelves for years. I'm the first one to look at it since the first investigation. That's not how we do things. John can't explain it. He would assign it to someone and that assignment seems to have been cancelled. Neither one of us can explain that." Dooley was frustrated at that.

"That's what I wondered. John had mentioned something along that line when he took over but he had no proof on that. It looks bad for him."

"It does but we'll back him. It's not his character to do that, unless we're reading him totally wrong."

"We're not." Aidan sipped at the bottle of water he had been handed. "How's Daci?"

Dooley shrugged. He had spoken with her over the phone but had not seen her in person. She had asked that he allow her the day and he had agreed.

"I spoke with her earlier but haven't seen her. She's hurting, Aidan, and part of it is because she can't help her ladies."

"That would weigh heavily on her, I know." Aidan was puzzled by what was happening there. "Dooley, has she said anything about being concerned that one of the ladies is not who they appear to be?"

Dooley shook his head. He had had a conversation just like that with Daci. She had looked at him, surprised, and then nodded. She had thought through the ladies and then shaken her head. Daci didn't think that any of the ladies had that character but she could not be certain. She didn't know the ladies well enough to know if one of them had done that.

"She doesn't know, Aidan. She's not as familiar with the ladies who are staying there as she was. They change every few weeks as older residents move on and new residents move in."

"That's about what I thought." Aidan was frustrated at that.

Dooley was on his feet as he heard a tap at the door. He opened it before he reached for Daci. Her face was covered in tears and she was shaking. It was totally unlike her.

"Daci? Love? What happened?" Dooley shut the door and then wrapped her in his arms.

Daci was not able to speak. Her sobs were too heavy. Aidan had appeared as he heard Daci's sobs and then was past the two to search outside and then search Daci's vehicle. He called for a patrol officer to head for Daci's and search that property.

Dooley finally just swept her into his arms and headed for the living room. He sat, his eyes on his beloved Daci, waiting for her sobs to lessen. They did not. He then began to pray audible for her, begging for this, whatever this was, to be over and that Daci could once more live a free life.

Daci gradually grew quiet, Dooley's prayers working their way into her heart. She rested back against him, grateful for a Godly man who loved her and who she loved in return.

Chapter 26

The week that he was forced off work flew by for Dooley. He spent as much time with Daci as she would allow, and it was a lot. He walked away from her home each time that he had spent time with her worried more and more. Dooley had not been comfortable that last day as he had walked to his truck. He stared at her home, knowing that he couldn't stay, that he had no right to, but wanting to. All he could do was pray for her and beg God to protect his lady.

Daci leaned against her door that night, knowing that Dooley had walked away from her with reluctance. She had had a long talk with Don the night before, trying to come up with plans that they could put into place if and when it became necessary. She had not wanted to do that. Don had simply planted himself in front of her and forced her to listen to him.

"Don, I'm not ready to do this." Daci was adamant about that fact.

"I know that you're not, but you need to listen to me. If you won't listen to me, then I'll bring in Richard and Abe and the three of us will face you down." Don was angry but not at his sister. She knew that.

"I know what to expect, Don. You've drilled that into my mind for so many years. What else do I need to do?" Daci refused to back down from her brother. They had locked horns before but not in such a life and death situation.

"Daci, I'm not saying this for fun. You know the consequences of what can happen. What can I say to get through?" Don ran his hands through his hair, looking past Daci at her comfortably furnished living room. The soft yellow of the walls helped to calm him down. He reached to hug his sister before he back away. "Just think over what I said. And call one of us. Any one of the men will help you."

"I know. They'll smother me and I'm not ready for that. Dooley is doing that as well. So is Aidan and Toryn. You guys need to back off some." Daci locked her brother out of her house despite his protests.

Don stared at the closed door before he shook his head. He walked back to his truck and slid behind the wheel. He could hear Delanie laughing softly as he did so. He gave a wry grin.

"Didn't go for your smothering, love?" Delanie thought it was funny even though she knew the severity of the situation.

"No, she didn't. Can't say as I blame her. We do tend to smother the ladies in our lives, even though they are all capable of standing on their own feet and fighting their own battles. It's who we are." Don grinned at his wife. "And you are correct to laugh."

"Sorry, it's amusing sometimes to see the two of you butting heads as they say. She's not backing down from you this time, Don. She won't. She's afraid and that fear is driving her to try and protect those she loves. And Dooley is stepping in, taking your place. She's letting him do things for her that she won't let you fellows do. She's in love with Dooley, and that's driving how she is reacting. She is also well aware that God is in control and is seeing His protection and the peace that only He can give."

Don nodded, knowing that she was correct. He just didn't want to walk away from his sister. And that would come at some point, he knew.

"You're right, love. And I have to step back and let her do this. It's part of growing up as siblings, learning to let them stand on their own two feet. It doesn't mean that I have to like it."

"No, it doesn't mean that, but you are wise to step back until and unless you need to step in. It's part of growing up as siblings, learning to let them stand on their own two feet. It doesn't mean that we have to like it."

"No, it doesn't mean that, but you are wise to step back until and unless you need to step in." Delanie hugged her husband before she walked away, intent on just what she had no idea.

Dooley stared at the white board three days later. He could see that Aidan had been around and added information. He frowned at that very information. Dooley had no idea how Aidan had found it, but he had. He turned as he heard the door close softly.

Aidan watched Dooley carefully before he walked towards him, his folders dropped to the table.

"Dooley? You look puzzled." Aidan stared at the white board as well, not sure what was up with Dooley.

"This new information? How did you find it?" Dooley's finger stabbed at the names. "I would not have connected them."

"Emma. She sent it to me and I think was sending it to you as well. To your work email."

Dooley nodded. He had not accessed that email yet that morning.

"I haven't looked at it and I should." Dooley sighed. "This is hard, you know. I want to be with Daci and protect her. But she doesn't want me hovering over her. She sent me home last night and told me not to come around today." Dooley gave a sheepish grin as Aidan laughed.

"Don't worry, Dooley. All of us guys have been told off somewhat like that. Daci is determined to remain independent and not rely on anyone. Part of that is from her training with Don. Another part is her fear that she will bring harm to you."

"She doesn't look at it in that I could bring harm to her. I get that. It doesn't change how I feel or what I want to do."

Dooley stalked away from Aidan, knowing that his friend was likely grinning after him. A small smile broke through the sternness on his own face. Daci had him twisted around her little finger and he could not go against her wishes. That was, not unless he had a credible threat that her life was indeed in danger. And if that was the case, he would just override her reluctance to have him near her and move in to protect her.

———

143

Aidan reached for the folders on the table, his eyes assessing Dooley. He nodded. Dooley, despite his worry over his lady, was concentrating on his task. He too took a seat and began working through the information that he had amassed.

"Dooley? You know that lady, Ella Evans?"

Dooley lifted his head, coming back to the present and the room.

"I do. I interviewed her. Why?" Dooley was puzzled by Aidan's question.

"She's dead. A heart attack." Aidan looked up at Dooley, shock on his face. "And I wonder if it was natural or murder."

Dooley reached for the report, reading through it.

"She had no history of heart disease. I wonder too." Dooley reached for the phone, intent on calling the coroner and asking some blunt questions. He had to be content to leave a voice mail for the coroner.

"It makes sense that she would die, doesn't it?" Aidan was frustrated. She had been their best contact to the murder and now they could no longer speak with her.

———

Chapter 27

Daci turned to face Dooley. She was not sure what he was asking.

"Dooley? What are you asking?"

"I love you, Daci. Will you marry me?" Dooley waited for her to speak.

She shook her head. She heard what he asked and had a good idea as to why. Daci could just not answer him. Not at that moment. His question was one that she would need to pray over. It wasn't something that she could answer that day.

"I understand that, Dooley. I can't give you an answer today. I need to pray over it." Daci moved into Dooley's arms, feeling his kiss on the top of her head and his arms tightening around her.

"I get that, Daci. I would marry you today but I understand that you need time. I'll grant you that and pray with you." Dooley had to walk away at that point, leaving Daci staring after him, hope in her eyes.

Daci walked through the downtown area the next day. She was searching for someone. She just didn't know who it was.

The street people looked at Daci and then moved in around her. Someone was trailing her, waiting outside of the shops and stores that she entered. The man didn't move in right away. He was being patient, waiting until she was on her own. Except that was not happening and that was not what he had planned for the day.

Turning as she heard her name, Daci waved at Shanli and Artis. They were two ladies that she had been wanting to speak with.

"Shanli! Artis! What are you two doing here?" Daci reached to hug them. She was at loose ends as she still was not back working.

"Looking for you. We are off for lunch and you must join us." Shanli pointed towards Ben's.

"That sounds like a plan." Daci moved that way with the two ladies. "I have a tail, ladies."

"Of course you do. We did." Artis looked around. "How do we get rid of him?"

"We don't. We keep stringing him along. I've managed to do that this morning with the help from the people around me." Daci grinned. "And I saw a couple of the guys from the team there." She sat, waving at Ben as she did so.

"They are great at that." Shanli looked up with thanks as their food was placed in front of them. "Are you up for a Bible study and prayer group tonight?"

"I am. I need that." Daci sighed. "Dooley wanted to come over but I told him that I had that group tonight. He wasn't very happy, I must say."

"He's in love with you, Daci." Artis gave a soft smile. "And you are with him. He's your heart."

"We are, Artis. We're talking." Daci was lost in thought for a moment, not seeing Dooley hesitating as he walked into the diner.

Dooley studied his lady, not wanting to intrude on the ladies. Shanli and Artis shared a glance and then waved him over. He grinned as he slid onto the seat, startling Daci as she shifted over.

Daci had thought that it was another of their lady friends, looking up to find Dooley there. He gave her a one-armed hug as the two other ladies laughed.

"Didn't see me?" Dooley shared a look with the other ladies.

"No, I didn't. You snuck up on me." Daci grinned at him. "I didn't expect to see you today."

"Word was out that you were wandering the streets and that someone was following you." Dooley's face grew stern for a moment.

"There was but the people moved in to protect me. It was a sight to see." Daci was grateful for their aid.

"I am sure that it was." Dooley grew silent as he listened to the ladies. He was puzzled by what Daci was facing and through Daci, what he was facing.

Late that night, Dooley sat in his office, his Bible open in front of him. He looked up at one point, a frown on his face. There was something that he was missing in the Evans investigation and he didn't know what it was. He had a thought and found a pen and paper to write it down.

He was at a loss to explain what was going on or to solve the Evans murder. He was at a dead end on that case for now. That frustrated Dooley. He didn't like having those cases not solved. Dooley reached for his phone, scrolling through his messages. He pulled up his emails but there wasn't one that would give him the answers that he needed.

Daci walked towards Don as he stood waiting for her outside his house. She had no idea why she was there. She had just felt compelled to find her brother.

"Don? Why am I here?" Daci hugged him and then stood back, focused on him.

"Daci? I don't know what you mean. I was wondering why you appeared." He swung her around to head for the house. "Delanie's working on supper."

"I'm disturbing you two." Daci bit at her lip.

"It's perfectly fine, Daci. You know that." Don hesitated for a moment. "We didn't ask you to come but you are welcome. I just don't understand how you showed up."

Daci shrugged. She had no idea why she was there. God had sent her. It was up to her to figure out why.

An hour later, Don reached for his phone to still its incessant chiming. He frowned as he read the text from Aidan. On his feet, Don almost ran for Daci.

"Daci? Aidan just sent me a text. Your house is on fire!"

———

Daci was on her feet, running for her car, before Don tugged her towards his truck. Delanie followed, the house door locked behind her.

Daci stared with horror at her home. Aidan had been correct. Her house was on fire and there would be nothing left when the fire was extinguished. Of that she was certain.

Chapter 28

Daci stared in horror at her home. Don stood on one side of her, Delanie on the other. They had their arms around her, watching the fire and then Daci. Daci could barely contain her sobs as her whole life disappeared in front of her in the hot flames. Smoke billowed to the sky, black and ominous. She was afraid, deeply afraid, almost terrified, Daci decided.

Feeling other arms around her, she realized that Don had called their parents and they now stood beside her, flanked by Don and Delanie. She couldn't look at them, almost ashamed to be in the position that she was in.

Aidan had searched for Dooley, finding him in his office, deep in research. Dooley had looked up, shock on his face, before he was moving towards his truck and heading for his lady. He approached her and simply wrapped Daci into his arms. Her hands found his as she refused to take her eyes from her home.

"Aidan?" Dooley turned to his friend. "What happened?"

"We don't know yet. Once the fire's out and it's safe, someone will go through it. There will be an investigation done, Dooley." Aidan was adamant about that.

"I understand that, Aidan. I want this over. This has destroyed Daci's life." Dooley was sober and devastated as he said that.

"We get that, Dooley." Aidan's attention turned to Daci. "Daci? What can you tell me?"

Daci looked up at Aidan, her emotions raw and open. She was angry. Aidan didn't think that he had ever seen her angry before.

"What can I tell you?" Her voice raised in volume and anger as she spoke. "I don't know what to tell you, Aidan." Her finger stabbed towards what remained of her home. "That happened. Someone burned down my home. I am glad that I was not inside nor was anyone else. Find whoever it is before I don't. It won't be pretty if I find them first." Daci stalked off towards her brother and his team, walking into Dooley's hug.

Dooley rubbed at his upper lip. Daci was angry and everyone in her way was getting the brunt of her anger. He never expected her to react this way but he watched her parents' faces and realized that he had underestimated her. They were not surprised at her reaction.

"You heard the lady, Aidan. Find out who did it." Dooley walked away to find his lady, seeing Daci standing and watching him. "Daci? Where do we take you?"

"To Don's, I guess." She gave a huge sigh, bringing smiles to the men around her. "I don't want to do that but I really don't have a choice in this. I won't go to Mom and Dad's. Don has better security." Daci walked into Dooley's arms, hugging him as he wrapped her tight in them.

"Don?" Dooley turned to her brother, finding him nodding.

"That's what we do, Dooley. Unless you two are planning on marrying one another in the next two hours." Don walked away, a smirk on his face, hearing the howl of protest from his sister. He stopped beside Aidan. "What do we know, Aidan?"

"Not a lot. I have officers reaching out to her neighbours. We're looking for home security video feeds as well. I'm not sure that we will find much on them." Aidan was frustrated. "This has been enough, you know. It was to stop with Kaelen."

Don gave a brittle laugh.

"It was and it hasn't. It's now my baby sister who is threatened. I want whoever it is and I want him yesterday." Don walked away, anger sparking from him.

Aidan had to agree with Don and Dooley. He wanted it over for Daci and Dooley. He just didn't think that it would be over very soon.

Daci paced Don's home that evening. She had sent Dooley away to his home. He had refused to leave her earlier. Dooley had walked away reluctantly, heading back for his office and the work that he had walked away from earlier.

Toryn paused as he watched Dooley before he too headed for his home. He was deeply worried about his officer and his friends. He didn't know how he could help them at this point, other than to pray for them.

Don watched his sister before he sighed. He had no words to speak to her. He prayed for her, without knowing what she would be facing.

Dooley walked through the board room, frowning. Where was the connection between all this? He had no idea but desperately wanted to find it. This, whatever this is that they were going through, was wearing both Daci and himself out. He had watched the others go through their adventures as they called them. He didn't want that for Daci but it was happening.

Turning as he heard footsteps, Dooley frowned at the man standing there. He was in law enforcement, Dooley decided, before he walked towards him.

"Can I help you?" He frowned as the man just stared at him.

"If you're Dooley, you're who I'm looking for." The man pulled out his badge and handed it to Dooley. "I'm Frankie Brennan from Riverville. I understand that you are investigating a cold case that we may have an interest in."

Dooley studied the badge before he handed it back to Frankie.

"Which one?" Dooley was not forthcoming, not yet. He didn't know Frankie although he knew of him.

"The Evans one. We have some evidence that has just come to light that may help you solve it." Frankie held out a folder this time. "This is what we have."

Dooley took it, flipped through the pages, and then stared at Frankie.

"Come in, then. Do you want any coffee or anything like that?"

Frankie shook his head. He had just had a two hour trip here and had a two hour trip home. That would be after midnight, he thought, and that would be a tiring drive.

"I'm good for now." Frankie studied Dooley. "What happened, Dooley?"

Dooley sighed. It had been a long day already and showed no signs of ending.

"Daci's home was burnt down. We think it was arson but we're waiting for the investigation. That won't happen until at least tomorrow." Dooley walked away from where Frankie was standing and then walked back to him. "I understand that you had an adventure as it's called. How did you ever do it?"

"Support from friends and my wife's uncle and aunt. Her parents were the ones responsible for what happened to us. And I was an undercover cop at one point, Dooley. That made no difference." Frankie gave a small smile. "And our faith. It was tested beyond what we ever expected, but God was there. He was faithful in His promises. And He is with you as well, Dooley."

Chapter 29

Dooley nodded, knowing what Frankie was saying. He and Daci had prayed the night before that their faith would be strengthened and that God would walk through this trouble with them. They were confident that he would.

"Frankie? What did you discover about this cold case? You didn't drive all that way for nothing, as they say." Dooley leaned against a table, his eyes on the other detective.

"The Evans case? We have a connection to them in Riverville. This person is not a criminal in any way, shape, or form. She has come forward to us, asking if we could look into the murder. She is a cousin of that Evans that was murdered." Frankie pointed at the folder. "All the investigations that we have done are there. I have left the names of two retired officers who would be willing to speak with you. One is the uncle of Abe Finlay, Eddie. The other is a my wife's uncle. He has so many contacts that none of us would ever find. Ben would be a good resource for you to speak with."

"Thanks, Frankie." Dooley glanced through the folder before he set it to one side. "It means a lot you taking time to come over personally. I might make the trip to your town in the next couple of days. Would she speak with me in person?"

"She would. Her contact information is included in the report. Bring Daci with you. You need to get away."

Frankie left not that long afterwards, worried about Dooley and Daci. He knew Don and his men and through them, Daci. He had not expected to hear of the destruction of Daci's home. That was a direct threat, he thought. Not the first time that this had happened to someone he knew.

Dooley walked away late that night from the police department. He was exhausted but equally just as worried about Daci. He had sent off a text message to her just before he left the office but had not heard back from her. Dooley had no idea where Daci was at that point in time. He would have to track her down the next day.

Daci rolled to her side in her bed the next morning. She was exhausted. Her sleep had been troubled. Daci had tossed and turned the whole night. Don had insisted that she come home with him and Delanie. She had been reluctant to do that but had finally acquiesced to that. She was hesitant to go to her parents, knowing that would put them at risk.

On her feet, Daci dressed and then headed for the kitchen. The coffee had already been made. That meant that Don was up and about. She didn't want to face him that morning. She walked out of the house and headed for her car, driving away to where, she had no idea.

Don stood and watched her drive away, a sigh rising within him. Daci was running, just as he had expected her to. He just didn't know where she was running to. Don suspected that she was running towards Dooley. His phone was out as he called Dooley.

———

"Dooley? Don. Where are you?" Don could hear the sounds of running water.

"I'm just up and making my coffee. Why?" Dooley yawned. He had not slept the night before. Instead, he had spent it on his knees, praying for his lady and for resolution of the cases.

"Daci is on the run. I don't know if she's heading your way or not." Don was frustrated, turning as he felt Delanie's arm around him.

"She might be. She might also be heading for the shelter." Dooley shut off the coffee pot, reaching instead for his keys. "I'll head out and see if I can find her." His phone was pocketed as he reached for the front door.

Dooley paused and then reached for Daci, wrapping her in a hug. He could feel the sobs shaking her body before he moved them to a seat on the front porch. Dooley didn't let go of his lady, instead tightening his arms around her.

"Daci? Sweetheart? What's wrong?" Dooley's voice finally broke through her sobs.

Daci leaned against Dooley, feeling safe. God was there, she knew. She also knew that God would never leave her or forsake her. He would be her protector and defender. He would cover them both in the hollow of the rock and cover them with His hand or tuck them close to Him just as a hen would cover her chicks with her wings.

"Dooley? Where do we go on from here? I just can't do it any more." Daci wiped at her face, trying to swipe away the tears. That didn't work out very well.

"I don't know, Daci. I really don't know." Dooley just sat, holding the love of his life. "Where are you going to live?"

"I don't know. I won't stay with Don. I can't do that." Daci sighed, a deep from the toes sigh. "Where should I live?"

Dooley bit at his lip. He wanted to marry Daci and take her away from all this. Only that would not solve anything.

"Frankie Brennan was through last night. Our adventure is tied to a lady in Riverville." Dooley shared that, knowing that he could.

"He was? It is? Can we go and talk to her?" Daci grew hopeful once more that they could resolve their adventure and resolve it that day.

"We can. I was thinking of heading there today. John is fine with that." Dooley watched Daci closely, seeing the stress that she was under.

"I want to come." Daci sighed. "But I can't. I have to wait for the investigators to go through my home."

"You do, but we can go another day." Dooley yawned at that. "For now, Daci, where are you going to live?"

Daci shrugged. She had no idea where she was going to live. That was in God's hands. Toryn had reached out the night before, offering her one of his rental homes. It was actually on Dooley's street, just down the street by about three homes.

"On your street. Toryn offered me the house three doors down." Daci's head went down on Dooley's shoulder and she slept.

Dooley stared at her in shock and surprise before a soft smile crossed his face. He knew that Toryn owned that home. He was just not expecting him to offer it to Daci. If she didn't take that home, Dooley knew that Don and his team would move in and put her into a safe house somewhere. She was not ready for that, not yet. It may come at some time but for now, they weren't ready to do that.

His phone out, he sent a text message off to Don, just letting him know that Daci had found him. He would take her with him wherever he ended up that day, likely to the office. Dooley was content just to sit for the moment. He really didn't have to go in and work that day. He had been told to take the day. He had not planned to but with Daci finding him as she did? That changed it. Dooley scrolled through his messages, hesitating on the one from Toryn. He sent off a quick response, asking Toryn for the keys to the house. It was furnished, Toryn said. All Daci needed to do was to replace her belongings. Shanli would make sure that there was food in the fridge. What else could they do for them?

Chapter 30

Toryn watched Daci late that afternoon. He had appeared at her new home, hugging her and then walking through it. Shanli had been around, he could tell, just from how Daci was reacting. He looked for Dooley, not finding him.

"Daci? You're okay with this?"

"I am. Thank you, Toryn." Daci eyed him as she came to stand beside him. "What can you tell me?"

"Tell you? About what is going on?" At her nod, Toryn looked down. He couldn't tell her. It was not his place to do so, as much as he wanted to. "I can't tell you, Daci. You understand that."

"I do. I was just praying that there would be some word. The arson investigator was in touch earlier, just before you came. It was an arson fire. I don't understand. Who did I anger so much that they want to harm me and destroy my reputation?"

Toryn's head shot around at her words. Did she really just say that?"

"Daci? What you just said?" Toryn waited patiently for Daci to respond.

Daci frowned at him. She couldn't remember exactly what she had said.

"What did I say?"

"That someone was trying to destroy your reputation?" Toryn was horrified at the thought. He reached for his phone, sending off a text message to Aidan.

"Destroying my reputation?" Daci nodded slowly, her eyes on Don and Delanie as they approached her. "That's what it seems to be. If my reputation is destroyed, then the shelter would close. We can't have that. Those ladies and children need it." Daci was sober as she spoke, knowing that it could well happen.

"I'm not sure if we were looking into that line of investigation. Aidan would know and I have asked him." Toryn was frustrated at that. "Who would want that?"

Daci shrugged, pulling a paper from her jeans pocket and then handing it to Toryn.

"Check out these names. They're all connected to the shelter board or staff members. I can't give you the names of the ladies. What I can do is ask if they are willing to speak with you on their own. Those who have moved on? I can't give information on them as we won't have it." Daci walked away from Toryn at that point, heading for Delanie who was waiting for her, bags of food in her hands.

Don had been listening closely to the conversation. He moved to stand in front of Toryn, almost matching his friend in height.

"Toryn? What you asked? What made you think of that?"

"It's the only possibility that comes to mind. Destroying the shelter building when she was the only one there? It would make it seem that she had done that. Burning down her house? It could be spun that she did that to throw attention from herself." Toryn had seen scenarios like this all too often. "And God is the only One who can protect her fully. We don't like what's going on with her and Dooley, but He is in control. That we have no doubt about."

"He is and that's where our faith comes in. It is difficult to walk through danger without growing discouraged or wanting to run away, praying that danger doesn't follow you. It is hard to wait for God's justice to be done." Toryn knew only too well the sentiments that he was thinking of.

"It is. But how do we do this then, Toryn? How do we prove it?" I think that Thomas was working on something along those lines. He was muttering about it yesterday."

"He was? Then he's realized something ahead of us once more." Toryn prayed for his friends, knowing that was all that he could do at that point. The investigation was going slowly and that frustrated Aidan. He also knew that Dooley was frustrated as well.

"Dooley headed for Riverville this morning, he said. Frankie was around with some information that he needed to confirm."

"I thought that's what he said to John. I pray that he finds some answers today." Toryn looked around as he heard Dooley's voice. "Dooley's here."

"He is. He'll have wanted to find Daci as soon as he could." Don walked away, heading for the outside.   He knew that Toryn had taken all the precautions that he could. He still had to assess the property and what might happen. That was who he was and what he did. His team would be around the next day, he knew.

Dooley turned from the living room window in his home late that night. He needed to sleep but something was keeping him awake. He was on watch for his lady. He finally turned and sought his rest, his prayers raising for his lady.

Daci was on her feet early the next morning, intent on heading for her brother's office. The team would be working on what was going on with her, she had no doubt about that. She shot a glance at Dooley's house as she drove by. It was early enough in the morning that it was still dark. There were no lights on. All she could do was pray for him.

Dooley walked through the down town area, knowing that someone or more than one someones were following him. He didn't care that morning. He wanted this over and this was one way he felt it could happen.

Stopping in an alleyway, Dooley waited for the men to appear. He didn't hear the man approaching him from behind. The sudden jab of a gun in his back had him standing still. His service revolver was pulled from his holster and then he was swung around and shoved towards the other end of the alley and then towards a building that housed a lawyer's office among other businesses. Forced to climb the stairs to the attic, Dooley waited for an opportunity to escape. That never happened. He was shoved into a ramshackle room, crowded with boxes and discarded furniture. His handcuffs were locked around his arms which were pulled behind his back. Dooley was shoved roughly to the floor before the men walked away, the door locked behind them.

Dooley sat back up, frustrated at what had happened. He stared at his revolver that lay on the floor next to him. He could not use it with his hands locked behind him. Only God knew where he was and only God could intervene to free him.

Daci paced that afternoon. Dooley was to have appeared and hadn't. They had planned on having a meal together out somewhere. This was not him. She reached for her phone, searching for any messages from him before she was sending off a text to Don, Aidan, and Toryn. Their responses came quickly, Don simply stating that he and the team were on their way, and was she safe?

Chapter 31

Aidan stared at the locked door to the board room, a frown on his face. It was only mid-morning and Dooley was scheduled to be there. Aidan needed to speak with him and could not find him. He reached for the door knob, finding the door locked. He turned, heading for Dooley's office and finding that locked as well. Frustrated, he headed for the desk officer.

"Joe? Have you seen Dooley?"

The officer turned to face Aidan, a frown on his face. He set down the papers that he had been holding.

"No, come to think of it, I haven't. He walked out of here over an hour ago." Joe studied Aidan. "You're looking for him."

"I am. I have some questions that only he can answer. Did he say where he was going?" Aidan was hopeful that he had.

"No, he didn't. He just waved on his way by and left." Joe frowned. "I thought that he was heading for the downtown area. He didn't go out through the back door and take his car."

Aidan sighed. He would now need to search the downtown area. And that was a huge search. Walking the downtown streets, he couldn't see Dooley anywhere. Arriving at Ben's, Aidan stood outside, watching the traffic around him. There was no sign of Dooley.

Walking inside, Aidan waited until Rachel was free. He didn't see Ben that morning and shrugged.

"Rachel? Have you seen Dooley this fine morning?" Aidan grinned at her.

"Dooley? Come to think of it, no. I know that he had planned to be here but he never showed up. I thought that he had been called out on an investigation." Rachel looked around Aidan. "And he's not here." She simply shrugged, not concerned that Dooley had not appeared.

"I was looking for him. I guess that I need to still search for him." Aidan wandered away from the diner, searching for Dooley. He was nowhere to be found. Walking back to the police department, Aidan headed for the staff parking lot. He nodded to himself. Dooley's truck was still there. But where was Dooley?

Toryn looked up from his desk at the tap on his door. He frowned before he waved Lyle, John, and Aidan into his office. This was not good, he knew, to have the three of them there and with those looks on their faces.

"What's up, fellows?" Toryn sat back in his chair.

"It's Dooley. He's missing. He hasn't been seen since he walked out of here about two hours ago." Aidan was frustrated and worried.

"He hasn't? And you've looked for him?" Toryn had no doubt that Aidan had done just that.

"I did. His truck is still here. He was to show up at Ben's this morning and didn't. I have officers starting a search downtown and looking for video feeds that might show him." Aidan rubbed at his face. "I have no idea where he is." His phone's vibration caught his attention and he pulled it out. "And Daci is looking for him. They were to have lunch together and he hasn't shown up. He wouldn't not show and not let her know that he wasn't coming."

Toryn was on his feet, heading for the board room. He unlocked it and then reached for the light switches. He walked through the room and along the walls, reading the information that was there. He nodded. Dooley was making progress, more progress than had been made ever before in that investigation.

"Now, where is he?" Toryn spun to stare at the other three. "Head out for the area, Aidan. We'll work from here." Toryn paused for a moment. "His beacon hasn't gone off?" Each officer had a beacon that they wore on duty, a transmitting device that would warn the department if the officer went down and stayed down.

By the time evening had arrived, the downtown area had been searched and searched again. The people on the street had been approached and all denied seeing Dooley that day. They would have admitted if they had. Dooley was kind to them when they needed it or even when they didn't. He was well liked by them, willing to lend them a hand if needed.

Aidan was frustrated. He was worried as well. He walked towards Daci, who stood near the diner, her arms wrapped around herself.

———

"Aidan? Any word?" Daci was hopeful that there had been.

"I'm sorry, Daci. There hasn't been. Not even a street person has seen him." Aidan hugged his friend and then stood beside her, his eyes on Don and the team standing behind her. Kaelen was there as well.

"How do we find him then?" Daci walked away from them, Kaelen at her side. She was searching on her own, stopping at each alleyway. She frowned as she paused at one before she headed down it. Something was leading her that way. Kaelen followed her. She could hear the footsteps of her brother and his team mates as they followed her.

Daci searched the area before she stopped in front of a building. She looked up at it before she climbed up the stairs and reached for the door. It opened under her hand and she walked through it, heading for the worn wooden stairs that reached to the top of the building.

Don moved past Kaelen and followed her, hearing the footsteps of some of the men following them. Others he knew would wait outside and provide a wall of protection for them.

Daci continued to climb, compelled to do so. Afterwards, she could not explain the impetus to continue up the steps. She stopped at a door, a hand touching it. She turned the knob and the door opened with a squeak of rusty hinges. Waving at the cobwebs that floated in front of her face, Daci stared around the room, seeing the jumble of junk.

Don moved his sister to one side as he and Aidan walked past her, starting a search. Both men knew that Daci would not have walked up to this door unless she had had a strong sense of knowing Dooley was nearby. A call from Don had Aidan rushing his way, staring down at Dooley.

Dooley had been attacked at some point over the day and was now lying unconscious. His beacon had been removed and then destroyed. There was no way that he would have been found easily. Aidan reached to unlock his cuffs and then reached for the revolver lying beside him.

Daci was on her knees, Dooley's head on her lap as she touched the bruises and cuts on his face. Sobs shook her body as she bent over him. Don stood with his hand on her head, listening as Aidan called for help.

Don swept Daci to her feet and then down the stairs, almost forcing her to leave Dooley. It was so necessary, he knew, but he didn't want to impede the treatment of Dooley or the investigation that Aidan was now starting.

The men surrounded Daci, providing a wall of protection for her. They stood with their backs to her, eyes watchful for anyone wanting to harm their friend. Don stood with his arm around her, Kaelen at her other side. Daci didn't move her eyes from the building entrance, waiting for Dooley to appear on his feet. Only, she knew that would not happen. Her prayer was for her friend and that God would heal him from his wounds. She had to trust God. There was no one else that would or could step in that way.

<hr>

Aidan stepped out into the hallway, frustrated and worried. He watched as the paramedics worked on Dooley, who had not yet roused or responded to anyone. He needed to speak with Dooley and determine what had exactly happened. He reached to help with the stretcher as it was carried down the stairs, Dooley's head moving slightly as he tried to rouse and then couldn't.

Chapter 32

Daci stared at the physician who stood in front of her, preventing her from entering the examination room. She moved so that she could stare past him, seeing Dooley still not moving on the stretcher. She simply walked around the woman and then approached Dooley, a hand out to grasp his. She knew that Joseph and Leah were on their way but they had been out of town that day and still had at least a two-hour drive ahead of them to reach Oak City. Daci simply refused to stay away from Dooley. He loved her, she knew, and she loved him. As far as she felt, they were a couple and no one would stand in her way to get to him.

The physician stared at disbelief at Daci before she made a move to follow her and remove her. Don appeared in front of her, arms folded across his chest. The look on his face stopped her.

"They're a couple, Doc. And they need to stay together. For now, they are under the care of my security team. And no one will deny that. If you do, then I go above you to the hospital head and he knows me well." Don refused to move.

The physician looked at him in anger before she stormed away, finding a phone to call for security. The hospital security officers showed up, saw Don and his team, and refused the physician's order. She was dumbfounded that they refused to obey her. She walked away, calling up the hospital head and complaining. Her words stopped as she was bluntly told that if Don was there on a security assignment, then he was there just to do that. The hospital would not stand in his way.

Don watched as she avoided any contact with him. A new physician had taken over Dooley's care. This physician was known to Don and simply nodded as he approached Don and then entered the room.

Daci listened to the physician, worried more than she had been for a few months, even more than she had been with Don. She nodded, her eyes on Dooley. Dooley had not moved since he had been shifted to the bed in the room. That worried her.

"When will he wake up?" Daci's voice was barely audible. Her prayers were rising for her fellow.

"I don't know, Daci." Jeff studied her and then studied Dooley. "His parents are on their way?"

"They are. They're about two hours away right now." She drew in a shuddering breath. "How bad?"

"How bad? How bad is he injured?" At her nod, Jeff sighed. "He's been beaten, Daci. There are no broken bones but he does have soft tissue injuries and more than likely a concussion. We can't determine if that is the case until he rouses."

Daci nodded. It was about what she had expected. Jeff walked away, hesitating as he passed Don and Thomas. He knew that the other men would be around somewhere, protecting the lady who they considered a sister and that their ladies were likely out in the waiting room.

Aidan was waiting for him, pointing towards an empty room.

"What can you tell me, Jeff?"

"Not a lot. He needs to wake up. His assessment is not complete until he does." Jeff gave Aidan what information that he could.

Aidan walked towards Don, a frown on his face. He knew that Don was there for a reason. He just didn't like that Don and his team had to be.

"Don?"

"Aidan? You're here?"

"I am. George is working the scene for now but I don't know that we'll find much information." Aidan was frustrated.

"About what you would think." Don turned for a moment, watching Daci. His heart broke for his sister and then Dooley. All he could do was pray for them. And that was the best that he could do.

Joseph and Leah had arrived during the late evening. Even though it was past visiting hours, they were granted access to Dooley's room. They were both horrified to find out his condition and that he was not rousing. They had no idea that he had not roused or that the medical staff had no idea how long it would take.

Daci had curled up in the waiting room, not willing to leave, desperate to know that Dooley had recovered. Don and the rest of the team hung around before the men other than Don had left. Don had found a seat where he could watch Daci and also watch the hallway to Dooley's room. He was convinced that something was about to break open and he wanted to be there to protect the couple. He just didn't think that was possible.

Daci's thoughts were muddled until she pulled out her phone and found her note taking program. She began to jot down her thoughts, as out of order and muddled as they were. She turned at last to her book application and found the digital Bible that she had on it. She began to read through the passages where God had protected His chosen people, knowing that His protection extended not just to them but to all who believed on Him. That was a promise she was clinging to. At last, her eyes closed as she slept. A passing nurse studied her and then found a blanket to cover her with. She nodded at Don as he watched her.

Dooley did not rouse the next day or the day after that. The medical staff were beginning to worry about him. Joseph and Leah arrived as soon as they were able to and left only when they had to. Daci was there as much as she could be. However, she was also haunting the down town area, trying to find out what had happened to Dooley. The street people were working with her but no one could find out any information. Whether this was deliberate or not, Daci was not sure. She just appreciated the effort that they were making. She was also reading over and over the promises of God to protect her and Dooley. That was a given, she decided. God was in control and had walked this path before them while walking with them at this time. She trusted Him to protect them.

Don was highly worried about his sister. He saw the dark shadows that were growing under her eyes and frowned at that. His team was working on the mystery, not getting very far. Emma was not finding out much information, which was highly unusual for her. Frankie had been in touch with Aidan, worried about Dooley. He knew that Dooley had been back to Riverville to talk to the Evans relative but he had no information on what the talk was about.

Hours passed with Dooley not rousing. No one could understand it. All were praying for him. Daci moved towards his bed on the third day, a determined look on her face. Today, she would attempt to make Dooley awaken. And awaken he would at some point, she was determined in that.

Chapter 33

The third day after Dooley had been assaulted found Daci creeping into his room before visiting hours. She stood for a moment, staring around. There seemed to be something evil in that room that day. She just didn't know what it was. Her attention turned to Dooley and she walked towards him.

A hand came up to cover her mouth as she struggled with her emotions. She had not come that day expecting to find that Dooley would be now intubated and on a ventilator. She wondered at that.

A nurse had entered after Daci, recognizing her. She did what she needed to, checking the equipment and then taking Dooley's vitals. She turned to watch Daci for a moment.

"Daci?" The nurse's voice held compassion.

"Dooley? He's on a ventilator?" Daci was horrified at that. "Is he that bad?"

"His oxygen levels are not staying where they should be. Once his oxygen level stays where it should be, then the ventilator will be removed. It happens, Daci. This is one way to help him heal." The nurse walked away, nodding at the officer who stood outside of Dooley's door.

Daci reached to lay a hand on Dooley's cheek, mindful of the ventilator. She drew in a shuddering breath, almost unable to control her emotions. She ignored the footsteps that she could hear approaching her.

Aidan had appeared, hopeful that Dooley had roused. The physician on duty had spoken with him, leaving Aidan shaking his head. This was not what he needed to hear. He needed Dooley awake and alert and able to answer his questions. He reached out an arm to hug Daci.

"Daci? You're here early." Aidan had no doubt that she would have spent the night there if she could have.

"I am. I was praying that he would be awake. Only he's not." Daci blinked back her tears. "Aidan? How does this affect your investigation and his?"

"We're working on them. George is working on what I was. I'm working on what Dooley was. We're gathering the information that we need and verifying it all. It takes time, Daci, as you know. Now, what can I do for you?"

Daci shrugged before she walked away. She had no idea where to go or what to do. She had to do something. She just didn't know who to trust at that moment. Daci walked from the hospital, not seeing the couple following her.

Doug and Darci watched Daci closely. Abe had asked Doug to bring material to Aidan and also to find Daci and Don. He was that worried about her.

"Daci?" Doug's voice caused Daci's steps to falter before she spun around to stare at him.

"Doug? Darci? What are you two doing here?" She sighed, her face turning up to the cloudy sky. "Abe."

"Abe. He was that worried about you." Doug reached to hug her. "Where are you heading?"

"I have no idea. I just want this over." Daci stood for a moment, her eyes on Darci. "Darci? You have a profile for us?"

Darci began to grin. She was a retired forensics psychologist but still did profiles for friends. She held up a folder.

"I did. We need to go over it. But first. Dooley?" She watched with compassion as Daci's face crumpled for a moment.

"He's on a ventilator, Darci. He's not waking up. And I need him to." Daci's voice held sorrow and dismay.

"He is?" Darci's arm was around Daci. "Come with us, Daci. We'll pray with you and then talk over what Abe and Emma have discovered. Kataleen's weighed in as well with a family tree for Aidan. She sent you a copy as well." She urged Daci towards Doug's truck.

Doug hesitated for a moment before he followed the ladies. He shared a look with Darci. This was nowhere what they had faced, with Darci almost dying at the hands of a rogue police chief, but it was serious enough that Abe had Doug head to Oak City.

Daci walked her home as Darci prepared something for them to eat. She had just shrugged as Darci asked if she could do that. Daci knew that Doug was walking outside of her home, searching for anything that should not be there. Doug was the lead officer on the ETF in Riverville and took the safety of his friends seriously.

Aidan walked towards Doug, surprised to see him there. Doug turned as he sensed another person there and then reached to shake Aidan's hand.

"Doug? You're here?" Aidan shook his head, a grin on his face. "Abe and Emma."

"That's right. We were heading this way anyway today. They asked if we could drop in on Daci. Somehow he knew that she would be at the hospital." Doug rubbed at his face. "Emma has sent on information for you. And Kat sent a family tree on the Evans. It is quite the interesting family tree."

"I'll take a look at it later. For now, I do need to speak with Daci. She just walked away from me earlier." Aidan turned towards the house, finding Daci waiting for him on the back patio. "Daci?"

"Aidan? What are you doing here? Don't you have something to investigate?" Daci turned and walked away from him, heading back into the house where she found Darci waiting for her. The two ladies headed for the room that Toryn had set up as an office. "What are we working on, Darci?"

"We are first working on prayer. You need that, Daci, to get through the next few days. You have no idea when Dooley will awaken and he will awaken. God is not finished with him as yet. We all know that." Darci watched with compassion as Daci wept for a few seconds before pulling herself together.

"I'm angry, Darci. I am so angry. I'm angry that God has allowed this. I'm angry that Dooley is not awakening. I am angry at the men who did this. I am angry at Aidan because he hasn't solved this yet. I'm angry at Don and the team for hovering and not letting me go out on my own. Does that sum it up enough?" Daci didn't know that Doug and Aidan had appeared in time to hear her.

"It does. God can take your anger. You are venting to your Abba Father. He understands even more that you can imagine just how you are feeling. I went through that as well. Doug, unfortunately, got a lot of the anger directed at him."

Daci jumped as she heard Aidan begin to pray. She hadn't realized that the men had appeared in the room. She listened as Doug picked up the prayer and then Darci. She was not surprised to hear Don's voice. Of course, he would have tracked her down.

Looking around at last, Daci sighed. Of course the whole team was there as were their ladies. Her home was now overflowing or so it seemed.

"Okay, Darci. Where would you start?" Daci turned to her, seeing Doug handing over a folder to his wife.

"We start with the family tree. And then we go from there." Darci was on her feet, making copies of the family tree for everyone. Handing them out, she found her seat once more beside Daci. "Kat did talk to me about it. Read it over and then we'll discuss it."

Chapter 34

Don was on his feet an hour later, walking from the office. He needed space to digest what he had been reading. Daci watched him before she followed him.

"Don? What did you discover?" Daci's voice stopped her brother in his tracks.

"The Evans from Riverville? I don't think that they are related to the Evans here. The family tree suggests otherwise." Don was concerned about that.

"That's what Kat felt. She was looking at another family named Evans." Darci searched through her paperwork. "Here. This is what she had found." She held up a paper, seeing the other searching for it. "Aidan? Where was Dooley in his investigation? I know that he was working on that cold case. He had mentioned it to Doug."

"I have no idea. I know what I'm seeing in his work. I just don't know what his thoughts are regarding this." Aidan rubbed at his cheek. "And I can't ask him yet." Aidan was on his feet, walking away from them all and heading for the office. He needed to keep working on the cold case even without Dooley to help him.

Daci watched him walk away, worried about her friend. Don shared a look with his team and all just shrugged. His attention went back to Doug.

"Doug? What would you do?" Don's question brought Doug's attention to him.

———

"That's a good question, Don. I don't know that I have an answer for you. I haven't lived in this town. I don't live your lives. I know that what we planned and put into place was against someone who understood only too well police operations."

Darci had turned to listen before she was nodding.

"That's exactly what we did. For you, Daci? It's different. You're not sure if it's someone after the shelter or after you. What I can tell you is that someone is out to destroy you and destroy your reputation. That way, they can take down the shelter. I would suspect that it is someone who had a family member go through the shelter and resented that they were kept safe. That person is high in your town. I know that you can't tell us anything and likely have no idea who it would be at this point." Doug was watching the two siblings closely, knowing that Don had been through a life and death situation and now his sister was facing that.

"That's only too true. Daci isn't sure how much the shelter is involved. We're not finding out what we need to and we should be. Even Emma is having difficulty and that is so unusual for her." Don was frustrated at that.

"Don? What if it isn't the shelter? What if that was just a warning and I am targeted by someone else who had access to it?" Daci was trying to think through it all.

———
182

"What makes you think that?" Darci was watching her closely, nodding as Daci was picking up on something that she had.

"It just doesn't make sense that it's only the shelter. I mean, I know that we have had threats over the years. A bomb is just too much over the top. Even with your profile, I can see them doing that to throw our attention away from where it should be. The cold case? I don't see that it's more than a distraction as well." Daci was working through her thoughts. "I don't know who to suspect thought."

Don turned as he heard a sound from Payten. She was studying the family tree. Not being from Oak City, she was reading the tree differently from the others. She had a finger on a name.

"This person? Is she still alive?" Payten gave a name, bringing all eyes to her.

"She is. Why?" Paul leaned against his wife to study the name. "She's active in town, on the town council in fact."

"She's the one, I suspect, Paul." Payten was adamant about that. "Daci? Has she had any contact with the board of the shelter?"

Daci hesitated, not sure what to say. She finally nodded, not saying how the woman had had contact with them. She couldn't. But she was not content that she was the only one.

Four hours later, Daci threw herself across her bed. She could hear her parents in the kitchen. She frowned for a moment before she realized that

Dooley's parents were there. They should be with Dooley, she decided, before she was on her feet, reaching for her purse and phone and then was sneaking from her house. Her car had been returned to her driveway by one of the guys. For that she was grateful.

Driving away from her home, she watched the car that pulled out and followed her. She frowned. She didn't know if it was an officer or an enemy. RIght at the moment, she really didn't care.

Walking through the hospital corridors, Daci headed for Dooley's room. She needed him awake and speaking with her. But that wouldn't likely happen. She was begging God to heal Dooley, stating that she needed him, but she also had to release Dooley to God. It was His will that was tantamount to what they were going through. He was the One directing their steps and walking that path with them. She didn't like what they were going through but they had to accept it.

Standing by Dooley's bed, Daci's face was sad. He was still on the ventilator and that troubled her. She felt as if he was dying and would leave her on her own. Her cheek touched his as she sobbed, her tears wetting his pillow as well.

Daci didn't feel it as Dooley roused somewhat. She jumped as she felt an arm around her but didn't realize that it was Dooley. Dooley had reached out through the darkness to pull his lady to him. His face rested against her hair before his movements stopped.

The nurse had watched from the hallway as Dooley had moved. She had not expected to see that, not yet. She frowned down the hallway before she was in the room, taking Dooley's vitals and switching off the ventilator to see if his oxygen stats stayed where they should be. She was surprised to see that they did. She switched the ventilator back on before she was out of the room and reaching out to the physician.

Don had realized that his sister was missing and searched for her. Thomas and Mark had headed for the hospital and arrived to find Daci sitting close to Dooley's bed, his hand in hers. They frowned at her for a moment before they realized that the ventilator had been removed.

"Daci?" Mark's soft voice roused Daci from her thoughts and her prayers.

"Mark? You're here?" Daci looked around seeing Thomas as well. "You're both here. Where's Don?"

"Waiting at your home. He knows that you need to be here with Dooley." Thomas looked at Dooley. "How is he?"

Daci shrugged. She really didn't know how he was. He had been removed from the ventilator but had not roused. She looked behind her, seeing Aidan there as well.

"Aidan? You're here?" Daci was on his feet, walking towards him. "What do you want?"

"How did you know, Daci?" Aidan was still working through how Daci had known where to find Dooley. "How did you know Dooley was there?"

Daci shrugged. She could not explain it. She had felt led by God to find Dooley and that was where He had led her. She just had to follow His leading.

Chapter 35

The next morning, Aidan climbed the steps back to the attic room to search it again. He had sought out the owner, who happened to be the lawyer in the building, and gained his permission to do that. Daci was beside him, knowing that she had to be there even if he had not asked her to accompany him.

The two stood for a moment just inside the doorway. The attic had been tidied up some, the boxed piled on one another and set in a more orderly row.

"What are we looking for, Aidan? I shouldn't be here." Daci rubbed at her arms, knowing that Aidan had wanted her there for a reason.

"I really don't know, Daci. I'm still trying to wrap my head around how you knew."

"God. He led me here. That's all I can say, Aidan. I don't understand it myself. I just felt compelled to come here." Daci stared up at her friend. "Again, what are we looking for?"

Aidan shrugged even as he entered the room further and looked around. He was puzzled why Dooley had been left there. He had searched the building history but had not found anything odd about it. He searched around the attic, not finding anything that would help solve the mystery.

Daci walked around the attic as well, not sure what she was looking for. Her eyes were on the floor, finding an envelope sticking out from under one of the boxes. She picked it up, seeing Dooley's name written on the front of it.

"Aidan? What is this? It has Dooley's name on it." Daci handed him the letter, watching as he studied it before he opened it.

Aidan read the contents, a frown on his face. It was not a threat. In fact, it contained information about the cold case, information that they didn't have.

"This is interesting, Daci. Someone left this for Dooley. I wonder who."

Daci had walked over to read the letter. She frowned. She knew the person who was named and had never felt comfortable around them.

"This person, Aidan? Are they involved in all this?" Daci walked rapidly from the attic and down the stairs, lost in thought. She knew that Aidan was following her.

"Daci? What are you thinking?"

"What am I thinking? That the person named is not one who I would have thought of. You need to investigate them." Daci stared at the buildings around her. She felt unsafe out in the open.

"Come on, Daci. Let's get you back to Dooley. He may have awakened and will be able to talk to us." Aidan's hand was on Daci's arm, propelling her towards his car and shoving her inside. She was in danger and he could feel in closing in on her. He didn't want any harm to come to her while she was under his care.

Daci walked towards Joseph and Leah as they stood just inside the hospital doors. Wrapped in a hug, Daci felt welcomed into their family. She frowned at that, wondering at it. Her parents had called her earlier that day, worried about her and praying for her. They had appointments that day that would keep them busy but they would find her that evening.

Dooley's eyes flickered open and closed that afternoon. He was gradually awakening, not aware of where he was. It didn't matter at the moment, he decided. He was tired and was in pain and all he wanted to do was sleep. He didn't hear his parents' voices as they begged him to wake up.

Leah turned into her husband's hug. She sobbed quietly, worried beyond what she had ever been worried about anything. They had been followed, almost too closely over the past few days. They had no idea when someone would attack them or attack Dooley again. They also worried about Daci but she just shrugged and went about her daily walk.

Dooley continued to move restlessly. Nothing seemed to relax it, nothing that was except for Daci's touch. Once her hand landed on his, his motions stopped and he slept. Joseph and Don had shared a look before Don nodded. Those two had a connection, he knew, that was similar to what all of them had with their ladies.

Daci walked away that afternoon. She was troubled, very much so, that Dooley still had not roused completely. He needed to awaken, she decided, and help solve what was going on. She walked towards Aidan who had appeared once more to speak with her.

"Aidan? Have you solved this yes?" Daci was hopeful that he had.

"Not yet. I need to take you to another building that has come up in the investigation. It is connected to the old shelter building." Aidan drove away from the hospital, watching as a patrol officer followed them in her car. He waved as she drove past him as he parked near another downtown building.

"The Grant building? They're related to the Evans?" Daci had not been aware of this fact.

"They are. It came out of Kat's family tree." Aidan reached for Daci's arm, keeping her in place. "We need to go through this. I have permission to bring you through, Daci, just because of what happened to the shelter building. We need to pray before we go in." Aidan did just that before they were out of the car and walking towards the front door.

Daci shivered suddenly even though the late-afternoon sun was beating down on them with a great heat for the time of year. She looked around, not seeing what was driving her fear. Someone was out there, she knew. She just couldn't see that person or persons.

Aidan walked through the front door, searching for anything that seemed out of order. He could not see anything. He could, however, feel the danger. His hand rested on his revolver as he walked through the hallways and then up the stairs. Reaching the top floor, he studied the open area. There was a door at the top of the stairs but the rest of the area was open. He walked into it, hearing Daci's footsteps behind him.

Daci followed him, a frown on her face. She had no idea exactly why Aidan had brought her there. She studied the area before she walked over to look out of one of the windows.

"Aidan? You can see the old shelter site from here, did you know that?" Daci pointed through the window. "Someone could have watched us from here without us knowing."

Aidan stood behind Daci, nodding. What she said was too true. And that disturbed him greatly. How this fact fit into their investigation, he just didn't know.

Neither one heard the cautious footsteps that crept up the stairs and quietly closed the door and locked it from the outside. Holding a hose to the crack under the door, he activated the container that he was holding.

Daci spun as she heard a hiss and then ran for the door, Aidan on her heels. They both tugged at the door, unable to open it. They began to cough as the fumes reached to them. Staggering away from the door, they both collapsed to lay in sprawled heaps on the floor.

A few moments later, the door opened and the men approached the two, gas masks in place. A jab from a booted foot flipped Aidan to his back. He didn't move. The men's attention went to Daci. One of them pulled her to her feet and then draped her over his shoulder before they walked rapidly from the room.

———

They didn't even bother to close and lock the door.
They would be long gone by the time that Aidan
roused.

Chapter 36

Consternation grew in the police department building as the officers realized that Aidan was not in the building. They searched for him there and then began to spread out through the town. He had been due for a meeting with the detectives and had not shown up nor called to let them know where he was.

The patrol officer who had followed Aidan looked around from her reports and then was on her feet.

"I followed him to the Grant building. Is he still there?" She was running for her vehicle and heading that way. "His car is still here, dispatch." She was out of her vehicle and running for the building, followed by other officers.

The building was searched foot by foot until they reached the top floor. They could smell the faint remnants of the gas or whatever it was that had been released. They stepped into the room. The female officer gave a shout and was on her knees beside Aidan. Calls were made for paramedics before the officers began a systemic search of the room and then once more of the building. One officer stared at the neighbouring buildings before he realized that there were no video cameras. They would have no way of knowing what had happened.

"Where's Daci?" The female officer stood by her car, facing Lyle and John. "She was with Aidan."

"She was?" Lyle had his phone out, calling the nursing station on Dooley's floor. He stuffed his phone back into his pocket. "She hasn't been with Dooley since earlier."

Consternation flooded the faces of those around. Daci was missing and Aidan was down and out of it. They had no idea what had happened and wouldn't until Aidan roused or Daci was found.

Hours passed as the search for Daci just expanded from the down town area. She was not found, despite the desperate searches made. The search was expanding to the outskirts of town, and then out of town with no success.

Aidan was slow to rouse despite the best efforts of the medical staff. Not knowing what he had been exposed to, they were not able to adequately treat him. That worried the physician who was searching for a treatment option.

Lyle walked towards Don, who stood just outside of the hospital doors. He had no idea that Daci was missing.

"Don? Where's your team?"

"At home. Why?" Don frowned at Lyle. "Lyle? What aren't you telling me?"

"Daci. She's missing. She was with Aidan at the Grant building. That's where she disappeared from. He had taken her there for a reason that he didn't say."

"The Grant building?" Don stared at him. "It overlooks the old shelter site. That's why. And the rumours are that whoever owned that building is connected to the Evans." Don's eyes slid shut as he struggled to control his emotions. "Any word on where she is?"

"Not a one. It seems that they were exposed to a chemical of some kind that knocked them out. And we don't know what chemical it was." Lyle was frustrated. "And we have no idea who was behind it." He turned as he heard footsteps. "Abe? Emma?"

"Don? What's happening? You are more than troubled?" Abe frowned at the two men.

"Aidan is in the hospital, poisoned by a chemical that we don't know what it is. And Daci is missing." Don stared at his friend and then Emma. "But you two are here?"

"We are." Emma reached to hug Don before she held up a folder. "This is what we've found. Where can we talk?" Emma looked around before she was heading for the hospital and the cafeteria.

Abe shrugged with a slight grin on his face.

"Emma's heading for the cafeteria, I would suspect. Come on, fellows. Let follow her before she comes back looking for us."

Don sighed. He wanted to be out there searching for his sister. He paused to send off a text message to his team and then to Richard. They would meet in the morning. The team that was in for training would get a crash course in searching for a missing person.

Emma studied her friend closely before her attention went to Lyle. She prayed for her friends, knowing that was what was needed.

"Don, we need to pray first." Abe was as good as his words, praying for his friends. He raised his head and stared at Emma who nodded.

"Don? Lyle? Where were they?" Emma was almost afraid to ask.

"The Grant building. Why?"

Emma drew in a shaky breath. Her reaction was not usual for her, Abe knew. He frowned at her before she shook her head.

"That was what I wanted to speak with you about. The owner of that building is the owner of the building where Dooley was found. It is hidden and I had to dig to find it. That owner is one of the Evans family. If I had known before, I would have told you." Emma was contrite at not finding it out before and saving both Dooley and Aidan from being harmed and Daci from disappearing.

"It is?" Lyle's notebook was out to take notes. He took the folder that Emma was shoving at him. "The information is here?"

"It is. It was important enough that I didn't want to send it by email or fax. Read through it. It has all been verified." Emma sat back and waited for Lyle and Don to do just that.

Abe looked around and then was on his feet. Richard was walking towards him, a worried look on his face that was not normal for the man.

"Richard?"

"Abe? What's going on? I was here in town for a meeting and got Don's message. Is it true?"

"It is. Aidan is down. And Daci is missing."

Richard drew in a deep breath. This was not what he wanted to hear. Daci was like a sister to him and he worried about her.

"When are we searching?"

"Tomorrow. I'm pulling my team in. I've reached out to some of my other friends who will be here. We need to find Daci, Richard. I fear for her life if we don't." Abe studied the darkening sky. "I just pray that she is still alive. From what we can determine, the person responsible has had a grudge against her for so many years and he is not adverse to her dying."

Richard shivered involuntarily at Abe's words. It was what they all feared.

"We'll be here. I won't find Don tonight. Tell him that I was around and I'll be at his place bright and early tomorrow with my team. Tonight will be spent in intercessory prayer." Richard walked away, a slump to his shoulders. He was highly worried about his friend and also for Dooley. He had spoken to Dooley's parents and was told that he was rousing but slowly.

Chapter 37

The next morning, Don looked around at the number of bodies gathered in the conference room in his office building. He sighed to himself. Delanie stood beside him, her arms around him.

"Don? Where do we start the search?" Delanie had spent the night in prayer, gathering with the other ladies on their team.

"At the Grant building. I've spoken with Lyle and John and they are freeing up officers to help. In fact, those who are off duty are arranging to search as well. I just pray that we find Daci today. I fear for her life, sweetheart. I really do. Whoever it is that is after her doesn't care if someone is hurt in the process."

"The ladies will stay here as will the husbands from Richard's team. Abe's team is here with their wives. I see Doug and Darci as well. Who all did he bring with him?" A slight smile cut through the distress on her face.

"Just about everyone he could think of, I would imagine." Don looked around as he heard his father's voice. "Dad?"

"We're here, Don, as are Dooley's parents. And the parents and siblings of anyone else who is here. It's a big group. Now start your prayer time and then sort out who is with who. We'll keep the home fires alight today for you. Joseph and Leah will be here until they can head for the hospital. Artis is there with Aidan."

"Have you heard how Aidan is today?"

David shook his head. He had spoken with Artis who had had tried hard to control her emotions as she stated that Aidan was still unconscious but was improving slowly.

The men and the two ladies on Richard's team sorted themselves out into groups of three or four and headed out to start their search. They were not optimistic that they would find Daci. They suspected that they would not easily find her and they were correct. Discouraged, they gathered back at Don's office building late that evening.

Don drew in a deep breath. The teams would be back on the next day but they had their own activities that they had to be at.

"Thanks, people." Don's voice held the fatigue and worry that he was feeling. "Let's pray and then you can head out."

Richard watched his friend closely before he approached him.

"Don? What are your thoughts?" Richard's voice had Don turning towards him.

"My thoughts? Right at the moment, I have no idea." Don was exhausted. Delanie stood beside him, an arm around her husband.

"Get some rest, my friend. I'll be back in the morning." Richard walked away, his hand reaching for Raleigh's. They were both deeply worried about Daci. Raleigh had expressed her thoughts that Daci might never come home and that had disturbed them both greatly.

———

Don nodded, watching as all the others left before he turned to Delanie. He knew that his parents were in the house and he hesitated to walk that way.

"Don? Where do we now search?" Delanie waited as he locked up the building and then just stood, his eyes on his keys.

"I don't know, sweetheart. I really don't know. I wish that I did." He sighed as he reached for his phone. It had been vibrating for the last few moments. He squinted at the screen in the dusk. "Aidan's awake but can't tell them much. Artis is worried about him and I can understand that." He scrolled to the next message. "Joseph said that Dooley is more aware of what is going on but still not fully awake."

"How safe are they?" Delanie walked slowly towards the house.

"I don't know. I wish that this was over. But God is in control. Daci is in God's hands, the best place that she can be. I just wish that she was home." Don reached to hug his mother and then his father, shaking his head at them. Both turned from him, discouragement evident on their faces.

Dooley roused during the night, feeling the weakness that crept through his body. He reached to raise the head of the bed, wincing as he did so. He stared around the room, noting that he was in a hospital and not sure why he was there. Dooley sighed. He threw back the covers from off of him and swung his legs to the side of the bed.

Waiting until his head clear, Dooley was on his feet, wavering as he moved towards the cupboards and then to the washroom. Dressing slowly, he then moved towards the door of the room. He stepped outside, not seeing anyone around him and walked slowly towards the elevators.

Sighing as he stepped out of the emergency department doors, he looked around. Dooley felt for his phone and called for a taxi. Walking into his house, he dropped to his bed, falling asleep almost before he had hit the bed. He didn't realize the consternation and disruption that was left behind him in the hospital room. The officer who had just stepped away from the door for a moment stared at the empty room before his phone was out and he called in for someone to check Dooley's home.

A faint light shone through the window of the door as the officer approached it. He received no response to his knocking. Lyle appeared beside him, a question on his face.

"Is he here?"

"I think so. There's a light on that wasn't when I was by here earlier. But there's no answer." The officer looked back at the car that stopped in the driveway. "Here's Dooley's brother."

"Daniel? You're here?"

"I am. God told me that I needed to be here." Daniel reached to unlock the door and stepped inside. "You're here for a reason."

"We are. Dooley disappeared from the hospital." Lyle stepped to where he could see into the living room. "We think that he's here."

"I see." Daniel walked through to the bedroom, seeing Dooley was stretched out on his bed. He sighed before he reached for a quilt to cover his brother before he stopped to pray for him.

"He's sleeping, Lyle." Daniel pointed to the kitchen. "It's going to be a long night, and we need coffee." He reached to set the coffee and then turned to lean against the counter.

"We do. He shouldn't have left the hospital. He wasn't ready to leave." Lyle was frustrated at that.

"No, he shouldn't have, but it's who he is. And once he finds out that Daci is missing, we're not going to keep him away from the search. And it will kill him if he's out there." Daniel sighed and then yawned. "Do we know who they are after? I mean, Daci or Dooley?"

"We don't have enough information to know that, Daniel. I wish that we did." Lyle stood, setting his mug into the sink. "I'm off to get some sleep. There will be a patrol vehicle and officer outside of the house for now."

"Thank you, Lyle. It is much appreciated." Daniel locked up after Lyle and then headed for the spare room. He stretched out on the bed, pulling a blanket up over himself. He began to pray for his brother and for Daci and then for anyone who was involved in the adventure. Then, as he had been taught to do, he prayed for those who he considered their enemies, the ones behind whatever it was that was going on. He slept, not hearing Dooley arising a couple of hours later.

Dooley stopped at the bedroom door, staring at his brother. He was puzzled as to when Daniel had appeared in his home before he shrugged and headed for the kitchen. He set a new pot of coffee and made himself some toast before he was heading for his office, plate and mug in hand. Dooley reached for his phone, plugging it in to charge it once more before he swiped the face of it and starting reading his messages. And there were many. The one that caught his attention had been sent from Daci's phone, a direct threat at him and her. He stared at it even as he prayed for his lady. He needed to find someone to help him but he wasn't sure who to turn to at that point.

Chapter 39

Daniel awoke with a jerk the next morning. He was on his feet, fearful that Dooley had disappeared. He searched through the house, stopping at Dooley's bedroom and then searching it. He couldn't find his brother. Heading for the kitchen, he felt the coffee pot, pulling back his hand as it was hot.

Snapping his fingers, Daniel walked through the hallway, his sock feet whispering softly on the hardwood floor. He paused just outside of the office, seeing his brother in his desk chair, an air of concentration about him.

"Dooley? How long have you been up and should you even been up?" Daniel sank into a chair in front of the desk, his mug of coffee hitting the desk top.

"Daniel? When did you get here?" Dooley looked up, blinking to clear his eyes. "I came home around midnight."

"You did. You caused quite the stir at the hospital." Daniel gave a grin at his brother.

"I did? I didn't mean to." Dooley sat back, his eyes on his brother. "You're here in my house for a reason. Spill."

Daniel gave a laugh before he sobered. Dooley had no idea what had been going on while he had been unconscious. He quickly spent some moments bringing Dooley up to date on what had been going on.

"That has all happened?" Dooley was shocked. "How is Aidan?"

"He's roused but I don't know what he has said." Daniel looked with compassion at his brother.

"Daci?" Dooley's voice was barely audible. He was afraid to ask.

"Daci? I have no idea where she is. None of us do." Daniel was highly worried about his brother's lady.

"Where did she disappear from?" Dooley reached for a piece of paper, grimacing with pain as he did so. He also didn't like the weakness that he was feeling.

"The Grant building. Emma and Abe were around. The owner of that building is connected to the Evans family."

"I know. I had discovered that the day I disappeared. I wonder if that's why I disappeared. I was handcuffed and left in the building. Someone came back and attacked me." Dooley stared at his brother. "What more can you tell me?"

"Not a lot, unfortunately. You would need to speak with John or Aidan, I think." Daniel yawned, his fatigue evident.

"I will." Dooley was on his feet, heading for his printer, and then returning to his chair. He passed over a number of papers to Daniel. "Read these over, Daniel. Tell me what you think."

Daniel read through the papers and then re-read it again. He nodded.

"Okay, so you've found more information on the Evans. Should I even be reading this?"

"It's common knowledge on the internet. I didn't find it using any programs that you should not have access to. In fact, Emma sent some of this on. She has been researching the Evans and the Grant building." Dooley searched through the paperwork, finding the report from Emma. "She warned me about them. I don't think that she expected Daci to disappear."

"We were all out there searching yesterday, Dooley. The teams are planning on being out there again today. Where should we be looking?"

Dooley shrugged. He had no idea. All he could do was pray for his lady. God would provide the information as to where she was.

"I have no idea where to start looking. It would depend on who took her. Where did she disappear from?" Dooley had not been told that.

"The Grant building. Why?"

Dooley frowned at his brother, rubbing at his forehead as he did so. A headache was beginning.

"Because it makes a difference, I think." Dooley stared down at his papers, not sure where to start. He sighed. "This isn't working out so well."

"No, it's not." Daniel's head turned before he was on his feet. Lydia had appeared and was working on a meal for them.

"Daniel?" Lydia looked past him. "How is Dooley?"

"He's hurting, Lydia. I don't know how to help him other than to find Daci." Daniel reached to pour their coffee as Lydia finished with the muffins and fruit that she was preparing.

"And just where is she?" Lydia stared at her brother. "How do we find her?"

"I don't know, sis. I really don't know." He turned as he heard the door once more and their parents appeared. He could see their anxiety but also something was up with his father. "Dad?"

"Son? Where's Dooley?" Joseph was looking around for him.

"In the office. He's been working away for a bit. Why?" Daniel frowned at his father.

"Because I think I know where she is. I need to speak with John or Lyle or even Toryn. Aidan isn't available and won't be for a bit." Joseph headed to find his eldest son. "Dooley?"

"Dad? What are you doing here?" Dooley was on his feet to hug his father. "You have news?"

"I think that I do. Your sister has breakfast ready for us. We'll eat. Then, we'll pray. Then I need to pick your brain."

An hour later, Dooley sat back in his chair, watching his father.

"Okay, Dad. What is it? What information do you have?"

Joseph nodded. He had spent time discussing the abduction with David and then with Toryn. He had then studied the building and the information that he had found. A friend from Elmton had sent information on the owners of the building.

"I spoke with David, Toryn, and then Samuel. Samuel did the title search that we needed. Here's the information that he has come up with." Joseph handed out the information, drawing an inaudible comment from Dooley. "Dooley?"

"This person? It makes senses. And Samuel has provided all the information that we need. Has this gone to John or Lyle?"

"It has. And it's gone to Don, Richard, and Abe. Those teams are preparing to move in and see what they can find out. They'll sort themselves out to find her. And that will be today."

Dooley nodded. He wanted to be out there, searching but he was enough of a realist to know that he would only hinder the search and not help it in his condition.

"How is Aidan? Has anyone heard?" Dooley was almost afraid to ask.

"He's home. But he's not working for a while." Joseph had spoken to Artis earlier that morning.

"I don't think that he will be." Dooley's eyes closed for a moment as he drew in a deep breath. His strength was almost gone but he refused to give in.

Chapter 40

Abe, Richard, and Don stood in the shadows of the trees that lined a quiet suburban street. They shared a look before their attention went back to the large, opulent house across the street from him. They had searched the surrounding area, finding the houses were all on large lots which were set quite a ways apart from one another. Emma had confirmed the identity of the man who lived here. Don had been shocked, not realizing that one of the shelter board had enough money to own this house.

"Emma's sure on this?" Richard just had to ask. He knew what the answer would be.

"She is. Daci is being held on this property. She just doesn't know if it's in the house or in an outbuilding. That's why we're here and not our whole teams. We take the brunt of any kickback and outcome." Abe had shifted to work mode as had the two men with him. "I don't like that we're on our own but it is what it is."

Don nodded. He knew the people from church and from what work that he had done for the shelter. It was not what he would have suspected but he had seen people who had hidden their crimes all too often.

As dusk, they watched for lights to come on in the house and none did. They shared a look and then ran quickly across the street to the shelter of the trees and hedges around the property. There was enough shelter for them to creep silently towards the house and the outbuildings. A look between them had them heading for the garage. Surprised to find the door opening on the end of the building, they crept inside, shielded flashlights lighting their way. The building was empty except for a couple of cars and whatever else was found in a garage.

The three men went building to building, surprised to find the buildings unlocked. That was not what they had expected, knowing how the man preached security and safety. Standing at the last building, Richard looked around. He pointed towards the house, the other two men nodding.

Don reached for the knob on the back door. He was surprised when it twisted under his hand and the door cracked open. He looked at Abe and Richard before they entered the house. They crept through the house, searching, and finding a room in the basement that was locked. Don reached for the key and twisted it in the lock. He shoved open the door, Richard and Abe's flashlights lighting the room. Richard gave a low cry as his light hit a body. Don was across the room and reaching to turn the body over. It was Daci. He simply swept her into his arms, his flashlight handed to Abe. The three men ran from the room, Abe stopping to lock the door behind him, and headed for Richard's truck that they had left on another street.

Don slid into the back seat, Daci buckled in beside him before Richard headed for the hospital. Abe had his phone out, calling Lyle.

"Lyle? We're heading for the hospital. We have Daci." Abe listened for a moment. "We did go into the house. The door was unlocked. No, there wasn't anyone there." His phone was tucked away before Lyle could say anything.

Lyle headed through the police department building, frustrated that the three men had entered the house. They could well be charged with trespassing, he knew. He would not lay those charges himself but it was possible that they would come.

Don slid from Richard's truck and reached for his sister. She had not roused at all, and that worried him. He nodded at the other two men, not realizing that his team had surrounded him and that the other two teams had spread themselves out around the hospital and in the Emergency Room waiting room.

Don turned in the waiting room as he felt an arm around him. His parents were there and Deree had reached to hug him. His father's arms came around them both. He had trouble controlling his emotions at that.

"What can you tell us, son?" David spoke quietly even as he maneuvered his family to seats near the door.

"Not a lot, Dad. She's being assessed. She was unconscious when we found her." Don bit at his lip, his eyes on Delanie. "We went into a house and found her. We'll likely be charged with trespassing."

"You are sure about that?" Deree had no doubt that Don had done that. "Whose home?"

"Evan Rogers."

"Evan? From the church?" David sat back. He knew Evan and had no doubt that Don would have been given permission to enter that house. "He and Jill are away and have been for two months. Does he know that his house was used for this? I can't see him being involved."

"He's not, David." Emma had approached them. "I spoke with him just a bit ago. He was horrified to hear that criminals had used his home. He will call Lyle and straighten that out. His concern was for his friends."

"He will? Thank you, Emma." David reached to hug her, his emotions too raw to seek more.

Daniel turned from Dooley's front door, opening it to find Toryn and Lyle on the doorstep. He simply pointed towards Dooley's office. They had had trouble getting Dooley to leave the room, forcibly removing him and sending him to his rest late the night before. He had been up and back in there before anyone else was up.

"Toryn? Lyle?" Dooley looked up, pain evident on his face but hope in his eyes. "You're both here."

"We are, Dooley. We need you to come with us." Toryn watched with compassion as Dooley searched their faces and then surged to his feet.

"Daci? You found Daci?"

Toryn nodded. He was not prepared for the hug that he received from Dooley nor was Lyle.

"When?"

"About an hour ago. We have her at the hospital. Don, Richard, and Abe found her." Toryn reached for

Dooley's arm to keep him on his feet. "Come. We'll get you to her."

Dooley stared at them and then down at what he had been working on. He reached to quickly gather up the papers and shoved them towards Lyle.

"Here. This is what I have found so far. It breaks open that cold case, Lyle. We'll need someone to prove it because I am too close to the case."

"We'll do that. George will take care of that. For now, come with us." Lyle waited for a moment as Toryn and Dooley walked away. He turned his head to study Daniel who stood beside him.

"Daniel?"

"Thank you, Lyle. This will help to heal him. How is Daci?"

"She's unconscious right now, Daniel, but being assessed. Come on. Lock up and come with me."

Daniel shook his head.

"I'll find Lydia and then head that way." Daniel paused in his actions and looked up, a simple thank mouthed to God.

Chapter 41

Dooley paced the hallway outside of Daci's hospital room. She had roused enough to speak with Lyle and give her statement before she slept again. It was early morning, just after midnight, and Dooley should not have been there. He had simply stared down the nurse and walked back to stand by Daci's bedside. His hand had rested on her cheek before he looked up and prayed for his lady. He had no words to speak. His heart was too troubled and sore.

Don approached Dooley a few hours later, a hand out to stop his pacing and then directing him to a chair.

"Dooley?"

"She's not waking up, Don. How do we do that?" He frowned as Don gave a quick grin.

"It was the same with you just a few days ago. You wouldn't wake up, no matter how much you were begged to." Don's eyes slid closed for a moment. "We need to keep you two safe, Dooley. How do we do that?"

Dooley nodded, knowing that Don was running scenarios and trying to come up with a plan.

"I don't know, Dooley. There are team members and officers around here and will be until Daci goes home. They are around you as well, whether you see them or not." Don eyed the man sitting beside him. "And I know that we will solve this and bring the culprits to justice. It's what we do and who we are."

"I know that we do. It's hard, being at this point." Dooley found his faith being tested beyond what it had ever been tested.

"Emma has sent on what she has. It's all that we need to close this off. It also closes off the Evans case as well." Don handed over the folder that he had set on the chair beside him. "This is what we have. I know that George is finishing off the case. You'll get the credit for solving it. It was your work that did it."

"I know. I'm not worried about that, Don. I just don't know where I'll work now. I loved being an investigator but I like digging into the old cases." Dooley's head went back on the wall behind him and then slept, his worry about the cold case relieved.

Don watched him and then looked around as he heard footsteps. Thomas and Paul were there as was Kaelen. He nodded at them, knowing that they had come to hold vigil with him and Dooley, watching out for the lady they considered a sister.

Daci was moved home the next day. She refused to go to be with her parents or even her brother. She was too afraid. The threats that had been hammered at her while she was half conscious did that to her. Daci was well aware that the men were around outside and that a patrol officer would sit outside of her door that night. The one person who refused to leave her was Dooley. He had simply walked into her home after her and locked the door.

Her stare down of him hadn't worked. Dooley had just grinned at her before he reached to hug her. She clung to him, sobs shaking her body. She had no idea how she had been rescued, other than the three men had found her. She didn't want to walk away from Dooley but felt that she had to.

"It's okay, sweetheart. It's okay. George and Aidan will meet with us in a few days and explain everything. Aidan is back at work part-time. I'll be back in once the case is over." Dooley turned her to walk into the living room. He was away and then back with a tray of food and juice. "Here. You need to eat and so do I. We'll eat and then I want to pray for you."

Daci nodded, crowding close to Dooley as he drew her close with an arm around her.

"When?"

"When? When will we find out?" He felt Daci nodding against him. "I don't know. I just pray that we don't face the monster before they arrest him. And that is a possibility, as you well know."

"I know. And that's what I'm afraid of. One of us would die if that happens." Daci yawned and then slept, relaxing in Dooley's arms as he held her and prayed for her.

Don and Delanie let themselves into the house about thirty minutes later, finding Dooley watching them with a grim smile on his face. Don's heart sank. Something had happened and that meant danger for the two in front of him.

"What happened, Dooley?" Don reached for the phone being handed to him. "What's this?"

"Read it. I've sent it on to both Aidan and George." Dooley was frustrated at the email he received. "It's from our adversary. He found my work email."

Don stared at him in shock and then down at the email that was open on Dooley's phone. His face tightened in anger.

"He's threatened you like this?" Don tilted the phone to show Delanie before he forwarded the email to his team and then Richard and Abe. "We need to come up with a plan to trap him. Aidan and George aren't going to find him."

"We do. We need Daci's input in the plan." Dooley looked down at Daci, finding her starting to rouse.

Daci stared at her brother before looking up at Dooley.

"Dooley? Where is he?"

"Who?"

"The man who kidnapped me. He won't let me go. He said that he would kill me first." Daci was so distraught that it took a long time to calm her down.

"Not if we can help it. We need to come up with a plan to meet him. He's sent a threatening email to me."

"He has?" Daci reached for Dooley's phone and read the email. "I see. What are the plans?"

"That is what we were just discussing. We need your input." Don leaned forward, knowing that his sister would come up with a devious plan. She had been known for that when they were teens.

Aidan pulled out his phone to read his email. He frowned and then began to laugh. He approved of the plan that Daci had come up with. It would be perfect revenge."

Chapter 42

Three days later, their plans were ready to be executed. Daci stood in the centre of a local park, on her own. The three security teams were tight around her, acting as just people out for a day in the park. Dooley wasn't sure that their plan would work but Aidan seemed to think that it would. George stood on one side of Dooley and then Aidan on the other side.

Daci stared around, sensing evil approaching her. She looked at Don, who nodded at her and then at Dooley, finding his gaze steady on her. She sighed. This was not how she planned to end this but it seemed as if it was God's plan. She didn't like it but she was willing to go ahead with their plans.

The man stood for a moment and watched Daci. He didn't see the men around her who were gathering close behind him. Don's team was the team that had been assigned to that task. He had wanted it any way. This man had caused too much danger and harm to Daci and Dooley. He would not let him get away with this.

Brett Evans walked towards Daci, the excesses of his life evident. He stopped in front of her, watching with a sneer as she stepped backwards, backing almost into Richard. He had chosen to be near her. His team was casually playing catch, their eyes watchful. They were ready to move in an instant if they needed to. Richard took a quick look at the man and then at Don and his team, a slight nod given.

"Well, well, Daci. You're here and on your own."

"What do you want, Evans?" Daci's voice was tight, her fear getting the better of her.

"You. You are coming with me. You destroyed my son's life and you will pay for that." His hands reached for her but she moved back from him.

"Your son? I don't understand. I don't work with men." Daci was truly puzzled at that.

"Yes, my son. You ruined his life. His girlfriend ended up in your shelter and then moved from town. She refused to have anything to do with him before she entered the shelter. That was your doing." Evans' voice was rising in his rage.

"I have nothing to do with that. They make their own decisions and choices. We just offer a shelter for them on a short-term basis. Your son? I have no idea who his girlfriend was. I don't ask for that information and we don't require it."

"But he said that you were the one." Evans lunged for her, missing her as Richard pulled her to one side and then handed her off to Stephen and Naomi.

Daci was rushed away, handed off to Dooley who wrapped her in his arms. Abe's team moved around them and then moved them out of the area.

Aidan and George moved in to arrest Evans. He fought them, a blow landing on George's cheek. His struggle didn't release him. He was handcuffed and then handed off to patrol officers.

———

Don and his team approached Richard, Aidan, and George. Don eyed Evans as he was hauled away.

"It's over, Aidan?" Don was hopeful that it was.

"It is, Don. It's all over. Let us have a couple of days to sort everything out." Aidan and George walked away.

Two days later, Aidan stood and watched the group milling around Daci's back yard. Toryn stood beside him. George was on his other side.

"I'm glad that it's over, Aidan. It's taken a lot from them." Toryn kept his voice low.

"It did. I wish that it had never happened, but like all of us, our adventure brought someone to justice. God protected Daci and Dooley despite how they were injured. He has been faithful in all."

Aidan was nodding before he was moving towards Daci and Dooley. He had explained how Evans had wanted revenge on Daci because his son's girlfriend had left him and then left town. He didn't count the fact that she had been the victim of domestic violence and had to leave to keep from getting injured or killed.

"Daci? Dooley? You two are okay now?" Aidan grinned at them, hugging Daci as she hugged him.

"We are, thank you. I'm sorry that you were hurt." Daci moved back into Dooley's arms.

"It's part of the job, Daci. You know that. God was faithful and protected you both. I'm glad. Evans will face a long time in prison for his deeds. He had someone plant the bomb at the shelter, set your house on fire and then had you two assaulted and almost killed. He's not going to be back on the streets very soon. He also the one who had that Evans murdered all those years ago. He knew that he was wanting to deed the house to the shelter and he was against it. They argued, he hit him, and the older man fell. The blunt force trauma killed him."

"No, he won't. And the ones he employed are facing some pretty serious charges as well." Dooley had had a long talk with Aidan and John earlier that day. He was well aware of the charges and the consequences that the men faced.

"That's true, Dooley. Now, will you two stay out of trouble?" He laughed as he walked away, his hand reaching for that of Artis.

Dooley looked down at Daci before he kissed her cheek. His love for her had grown more and more each day. Daci looked up at him, her love for him on her face.

A year later, Daci moved among almost the same group. They had arranged a Saturday lunch for them, grateful that they were all able to meet in Dooley's backyard. It was a perfect sunny day, the temperature just right with a light breeze blowing. She turned as she felt an arm come around her and reached to accept Dooley's kiss. They had married three months after their adventure had ended.

Daci had decided that she no longer wanted to lead the shelter work but had stayed on as a counsellor. That was where she worked best, she stated.   The shelter had been rebuilt and expanded and now helped even more women and children than they had before. An off-shoot program had set up foster care for any pets that the ladies brought with them. This had been a dream of Daci's for years.

"Okay, sweetheart?" Dooley's voice was low but held the love that he had for her.

"I am, my love. I am. It's been good for all of us."

Daci and Dooley had a secret that they were not yet ready to share. They would be parents in a few months. For now, they were hiding that fact just to enjoy it themselves.

Daci's eyes searched through the people, seeing the young children and babies that were there. She was grateful for that.   She thought of the verses that mentioned the mothers bringing their children to Jesus for His blessing. Her face glowed as those thoughts flowed through her mind.

She found Don standing with Richard. Both men held small babies, Don with his daughter and Richard with his son. They were both only a month or so old, but Daci loved both of the babies.

"Don's happy as is Richard." Daci's quiet voice only reached Dooley's ears.

"They are. God has greatly blessed us, not just with work, but with family and friends. Our friends' group is growing, sweetheart, and I would miss not having any one of them in our lives."

"They are great friends. The guys tend to smother us or did until we found our life mates. God has been gracious and faithful for all of us. There were times that I doubted Him and grew angry. He was able to take my emotions and turn them into praise for Him. I don't know how people without faith get by in danger and illness and whatever it is that we face."

Don's eyes found his sister even as he handed over his daughter to Delanie. He knew that their parents were around somewhere and that little Dee as she was called would end up with his mother or father. He was happy with Dooley in his sister's life. They were meant for one another.

Richard watched Don and then Daci. They had been friends for so many years and had been through a lot together. He could only thank God that He had protected all of them and brought them through the danger that they had faced. He prayed his prayer of praise with his usual ending of I love You.

———

224

That evening, Dooley searched for Daci, finding her settled on the back deck in the glider that she favoured. He sat beside her, an arm wrapped around her. His hand rested on her abdomen for a moment even though he knew it was too soon to feel the movements of the baby.

"Okay, sweetheart?" Dooley's voice was once again low.

"I am. And you?"

Dooley nodded. That day had been tiring but they had needed to meet as they had. It had been a trying year but they had watched God at work in their lives and the lives around them.

"Are you okay with staying working on the cold cases?"

"I am. It is quite interesting and to solve them gives closure to the families that they don't have. And you? You're okay not running the shelter?" Dooley watched her beloved face closely.

"I am, Dooley. I was stressed way too much running the shelter. Joyce is where she wants to be taking over for me. She's the one God will use. Our church is healing as well." Daci grew quiet, her head on Dooley's shoulder, feeling safe, cherished, and loved.

Thank you for reaching for the story of Daci and Dooley. Once more, the characters have just let me type out their story. They told it, just letting me know as I typed. Who the culprit is has always been a surprise for me.

Their path into danger proved that their faith in God was true and strong. God was shown to be gracious and faithful and steadfast in protecting them. He is that way for us as well. My father always maintained that we never know what danger or illness we have avoided due to God's protection. He was so correct in that.

Now, the people who joined in the story. Don and his team are in His Protectors. Richard and his team are in His Defenders. Abe and his team are in His Guardians. Samuel and his friends are in His Guardians. Doug and Darci's story can be found in The Heart of a Lion. Frankie and Deirdre's are in The Storm, book one of The Haven of Rest. They like to walk back and forth in the stories. When Abe and Emma appear, the story always moves forward. Aidan's story is in Aidan. Kaelen's is Kaelen. Toryn is Toryn. Barnabas Carey is part of The Barnabas Chronicles.

Once more, trust God in your daily walk. He has walked the path before you. He desires on His best for you.

God bless.

Ronna